THE HOTEL MAGNATE'S DEMAND

BY
JENNIFER RAE

Harlequin (UK) Limited's policy is to use papers that are natural,
renewable and recyclable products and made from wood grown in
sustainable forests. The logging and manufacturing processes conform
to the legal environmental regulations of the country of origin

Printed and bound in Spain
by ... S.A., Barcelona

MILLS
BOON®

Published in Great Britain 2015
by Mills & Boon, an imprint of Harlequin (UK) Limited,
Eton House, 18-24 Paradise Road, Richmond, Surrey, TW9 1SR

© 2015 Jennifer Rae

ISBN: 978-0-263-24872-2

Harleq... ...ers that are natur...
renewa... ...e p... ...made from wood grow... ...n
sustain... ...manufacturing processes ... ...form
to the l... ...of the country of origin

Printed ...
by CPI...

THE HOTEL
MAGNATE'S
DEMAND

This book is for the boys in my life.

For the boys who loved me when I wasn't very lovable,
the boys who cheered me up when I was feeling down,
and the boys who took care of me when I needed it.

I'm grateful for you all.

But mostly this book is dedicated to the two boys
who mean more to me than any other boy
ever has or ever will.

To Archie and Max

The two boys I love the most.

CHAPTER ONE

THREE MILLION DOLLARS. The sweet, stupid lunatics at Amy McCarthy's work were seriously trusting her with *three million dollars*? No matter how many times it happened Amy was still amazed that she'd managed to convince people she knew what she was on about. Didn't they know that she was a five-year-old dressed in a twenty-six-year-old's clothing? If they had, perhaps they wouldn't have opened that bottle of champagne tonight and toasted her success.

Perhaps they wouldn't have told her how proud they were of her for landing the biggest account in the company's history. Perhaps they would have done what they should have and handed the account to Maree, or Thomas, or another of one of the senior PR consultants. The grown-ups. The sensible, reliable, practical grown-ups who knew what the hell they were doing. Not her. Who considered it a win when she managed to find matching socks to wear to the gym.

The grin on Amy's face was almost manic as she pushed open the heavy door to Saints, the hip bar and restaurant in Surry Hills where she was meeting the others. Seriously. She totally had no idea what she was supposed to do with these new clients. They were the biggest luxury hotel chain in the entire Asia Pacific region.

She knew nothing about hotels! She was all talk. She knew that. She'd been able to sweet-talk people into anything since she was little. She'd even considered using her sales ability as her talent when she'd entered the Miss Northern Suburbs competition in high school. But she'd gone with magic instead. Which was probably why she'd lost. Either that or the fact that she'd been the dumpiest, plumpest, most unfashionable girl in the competition.

Amy remembered the long flowing bohemian dress she'd chosen for the 'formal wear' part of the competition. She'd loved it. It had made her feel pretty and feminine and free. But the judges had called her a hippy, and apparently hippies didn't win beauty contests. So she'd lost. But her mother had hugged her and told her she was cleverer than those silly judges and her father had insisted she was the most beautiful girl there.

Her parents were two more sweet, silly people in her life. Thinking she was so much brighter and cleverer and better than she actually was.

Perhaps that was why, Amy thought, she had a tendency to make bad decisions. Too many people telling her she could do anything. Maybe she needed to surround herself with some more realistic people.

Grounded, sensible people, who didn't hope for the impossible but had their feet firmly set on the ground.

People like Willa. Amy spotted her best friend as soon as she alighted from the small flight of stairs that led to the dark bar that had become her local in recent months. Willa's bright smile caught on the light and Amy smiled. Funny, clever, crazy Willa.

Amy couldn't wait to tell her friend about her latest mad scheme. Of course Amy would exaggerate and make it seem even more outrageous than it actually was. She knew that would make Willa laugh and she loved to make Willa laugh. Because that made Amy laugh and there was nothing Amy liked to do more than laugh. And go out. And work. And stay as busy as possible. Staying busy meant staying high. And staying high meant not thinking about things that made her sad.

A familiar fleeting pull swept through Amy's stomach. It shot up her body like a firecracker, passed her brain and went straight for her eyes. Amy stilled. Gulped. Then shook her head. Shook the feeling away. Where had *that* come from? There was no time for sadness. No time for thinking about anything that made her unhappy. No time for thinking about all the people she'd hurt or those people who had hurt her. She wanted to have fun. She wanted to laugh. She needed to talk to Willa. Now.

With a somewhat forced skip in her step she headed for the banquette that held Willa and her boyfriend, Rob, as well as their other friends, Scott, Kate, Chantal, Brodie and Jess. Amy counted them all off in her head, knowing she was the last one to arrive. She was often the last one to arrive these days. Work was becoming more manic as she took on more clients but that was the way she liked it. Busy.

Amy stilled. She counted her friends' heads again. There should be seven. But there were eight. Another head. An unfamiliar head. A male head with its back turned towards her. Amy wondered for a moment who the newcomer was. Their group was pretty tight. Newcomers weren't usually a thing, and if anyone was to introduce anyone it was usually her.

Amy's eyes skirted to Jess, who was looking at the newcomer with a strange, faraway look in her eye. *Aha!* That was it. Jess had invited a man. But that didn't make any sense, because Amy had spoken to her this morning before dashing out through the door and Jess hadn't said anything about a man.

Not that she had time to worry about Jess and her man or anything else. She'd won a massive contract. There were tales to tell and cocktails to be ordered.

Amy swung the Louis Vuitton bag she'd splurged on with her last bonus cheque onto the low seat the strange man happened to be sitting on and used her best PR voice.

'Ladies and gentlemen, hold your applause, but I must inform you that you are about to share copious amounts of alcohol with Bird Marketing's newest superstar.'

Everyone looked up and smiled at her encouragingly. Amy focussed on Willa, barely containing her need to say something outrageous and make her laugh. Willa had a strange smile on her face. A smile that wasn't quite a smile. And her eyes kept looking downward, then scooting back up. What was she *doing*?

'And, furthermore, I've managed to convince the idiots in charge that allowing me full control of their newest and most important client as well as their three million dollars was the best bloody idea they've ever had.' Amy laughed.

Scott stood and gave her a hug. Jess squealed in delight and called out congrats, and Brodie said loudly that her bosses must be nut-jobs.

Strangely, though, Willa didn't move. She smiled a tight smile. Frankly, Amy had expected more. A laugh, a joke, a call for drinks all round. But Willa sat still, that silly strange smile still planted on her face and her eyes now frantically moving up and down.

'Amy…' she started, finally getting up from her seat.

Her eyes were still scooting down and Amy finally realised where she was looking. At the stranger. Who Amy could now feel was looking at *her*. So Amy looked back. Then she looked at Willa. Who had stopped still. As had Amy. Her brain seized. Every cell in her body froze. No air was being released from her lungs and she was pretty sure her heart had actually stopped beating.

'Ames…'

Willa again. Amy willed herself to breathe. She felt the warmth of her best friend's hand on her arm and she was grateful for it. Because right at the moment she wasn't sure that she wouldn't faint. Her knees gave a little as her eyes met Willa's, holding them steady.

A conversation went on between the two friends without one word being spoken. A telepathic conversation that they had a knack for.

Is it?

Calm down.

No. Tell me it can't be.

Hold steady. It'll be okay.

I'm not prepared. What did I say? Did I make a fool of myself?

Just look at him.

So Amy did. She looked down at him. But right at that moment he stood. All six feet of him. Tall. Solid. Strong and dark. Amy forced herself to swallow and made her eyes trail up his chest, past his broad shoulders and to his face. A face she thought she'd forgotten. A face she'd never forget. It was him. He was here. In the flesh.

Luke.

Amy tried to speak but nothing came out. She tried again. She knew what she wanted to say. She'd practised what she wanted to say. Ever since she'd got back in contact with her old friend Willa months ago she'd been going over and over what she might say should she meet Luke, Willa's brother, her former boss and the man she'd had the fiercest crush of her life on. Who also happened to be one of only two people who knew her deepest, darkest secret. But all those words were gone. Somewhere. In the ether.

'Hello, Amy. It's been a long time.'

Yes, it has. Hello, Luke. Nice to see you. How are you? There were any number of things Amy could have said right at that moment. She dug her nails into Willa's flesh and jerked her friend towards her.

'I'm…gonna go get a drink.' Then she turned and fled, pulling her poor friend with her.

'Now, Amy, before you lose it…'

'*Before* I lose it? Before I *lose* it? Willa—I've already lost it! Why didn't you tell me Luke was coming? You should have warned me!'

'He literally just landed today and texted me. I told him to come along but honestly I didn't think he would.'

'Oh, God, what did I say? I can't even remember.'

As was the norm whenever Luke was around, Amy became a little ditzy. That logical, clever part of her brain evaporated when she saw him. Which was crazy. It had been—what? Seven years? No. Eight. Eight years since she'd seen him. Eight years since that night. The swooping roared through her stomach again.

Amy pulled her face into a smile.

'Okay—that's okay. It's fine. I'm fine. I was just shocked, you know…? I want to see him. I'm happy to see him. Let's get a drink—what are you drinking? Actually. drinks all round! We're celebrating. remember?'

Willa's eyes were soft, her expression so readable.

'Don't look at me like that, Willa. I'm fine.' Amy

said it firmly. With one of her signature smiles. Before turning to the bearded, tattooed bartender.

'Dave, darling. You look hot tonight! Sweet haircut. Sharp.' She smiled with all her teeth and winked. It was the smile she used when she wanted people to smile back.

She wanted everyone smiling tonight. She wanted everyone talking and happy. She needed her heartbeat to return to normal so she could turn around and face Luke. She wasn't even sure what she was getting so wound up for. Luke was an old friend—that was all. Sure, she'd had some silly little crush on him once. But that had been years ago. She'd only been eighteen then. A teenager.

She was a woman now. With a lot more confidence and plenty more experience. She'd changed. She'd moved on. And she was sure he had too. He probably barely remembered her. Or what had happened. That feeling again. Swooping through her. Every time she thought that feeling had finally disappeared a night like this would come. A night when it would return and lurk and keep tapping at her like an insistent salesman at a door.

'*Go away!*' she whispered to herself.

'Not exactly a warm welcome. I've only just got here.'

Amy felt him before she saw him. His warm, dark presence behind her. That slightly gruff and very deep voice in her ear. When she was eighteen it had made her melt and giggle. But today she wasn't melting. She wasn't giggling. She'd just landed a highly cov-

eted three-million-dollar PR account, for God's sake.
She was strong and powerful and in control. Strong,
powerful women didn't melt.

But Amy grabbed the bar anyway—just in case.

'I wasn't talking to you.' Her voice came out all
breathy and high. *Dammit.* Amy schooled it into
something deeper. Her best PR voice. 'How have you
been, Luke? It's been for ever!'

'Eight years.'

Luke didn't move. Amy had used to love that about
him. How he was so still and solid. Big. Brave. Everything she wasn't.

At best she remembered herself as being flaky
during the months she'd spent working at Weeping
Reef as a receptionist for the tropical resort. At worst
selfish, self-centred and a right little brat. No wonder Luke wasn't smiling. She'd always been his little
sister's troublemaking friend. He'd never seen her
as anything but that. And she'd always seen him as
Willa's annoyingly controlling big brother. *Hot* big
brother. As in smoking hot.

And right now, up close, Amy realised that hadn't
changed. Actually, if anything, he was even hotter.
He'd always been tall, but now he'd filled out more.
His jaw was wider, his shoulders broader. His voice
was even deeper. His hair was still thick and dark, but
it was clipped a lot shorter than in the old days, when
unruly curls had fallen carelessly over his forehead.

And gone were the board shorts and the resort polo
shirts he'd used to wear. Luke stood tall in an expen-
sive-looking suit. Complete with tie. Somehow, even

though he looked a little restrained by all the neatness and correctness, it suited him. It definitely suited the grim look on his face.

Amy lifted her eyes to his. His eyes were still the same. Green. They were like those old mood rings they'd used to peddle in the gift shop. When he was happy they'd turn bright, like the Whitsunday ocean, and when he was angry or upset they'd come over a shade of stormy dark green. She remembered the stormy green. Luke had always seemed to be upset with her over one thing or another. But she'd only ever seen them violently green once. That one time…

Amy clung to her stomach, willing it not to swoop again. She didn't want that unwelcome feeling to reach her eyes as it threatened to do each time. She wouldn't cry. She'd *never* cry over that. Not again.

'Eight years. Wow. And still looking over our shoulders, ruining all our fun.' Amy smiled, hoping he'd take her words as she'd meant them—teasingly.

'And by the looks of it you two haven't changed much either. Still giggling over boys and drinking too many cocktails.'

Something resembling a smile lifted the corner of his mouth and he flicked his suit jacket back to push his hands into his pockets. He got it. He got *her*. He always did.

'You just wish we were giggling over *you*.' Amy smiled again. She couldn't help it.

She'd always liked to tease Luke. She'd always pushed and pushed till the grim look on his face cracked into a smile. It was a game she'd enjoyed playing when she was eighteen and had had her whole life in front of her. Now, at twenty-six, she should be more cautious. She should have learned a few lessons. But it seemed with Luke she was still clueless. Because flirting with him felt good. *Still.*

'I'm sure you are.'

He leaned in and Amy caught his scent. The same fresh, oceany goodness that she remembered. His lips brushed her cheek just lightly. As if he was afraid to go near her.

Amy was grateful. It was important to keep her distance. Especially with Luke. There was no doubt she'd been looking forward to seeing him again. She'd thought about it often since rekindling her friendship with Willa. She'd asked Willa about him a few times. Subtly. Without letting on to her friend how she felt.

Not that she was *sure* how she felt. Luke was someone from her past. Her very long ago past. And even then he hadn't been anything to her…just a crush. And she hadn't been anything to him. Just his sister's silly little friend. An idiot who'd needed rescuing.

Amy clutched at her stomach and turned back to the bar, where Dave was now racking up the drinks. She smiled, she flirted, she paid all her attention to Dave. So much so that she could see him blushing underneath his beard. Her stomach settled. Her heart returned to normal. She wouldn't think of that night. She wasn't sure why she kept thinking of it—she'd learned to block it out years ago.

Maybe it was because Luke was here. And he smelled the same. She still remembered breathing him in as he carried her out to the Jeep and took her to the hospital. She remembered clinging to him shamelessly as he laid her in the back seat.

'Don't leave me.'

'I'm not. I'm right here. But I have to drive.'

'No!' The tears from her eyes had met her still wet cheeks. 'Please. Just hold me.'

She'd been irrational. She'd known that at the time. But she hadn't been able to help it. For those three minutes the fact that his arms were around her had been the only thing stopping her from collapsing, and she'd been convinced she'd stop breathing if he let her go.

He'd reached for her hair, stroked it back off her forehead. Then with one finger he'd traced the cut in her lip. She hadn't winced. His touch had soothed the pain. She'd clung to his hand.

'No one is going to hurt you again, Amy. I promise you.'

'But…'

'Amy—look at me.'

That was when she'd seen his eyes so violently green.

'I *promise* you.'

She'd believed him. She'd looked into his eyes and into his soul and seen her protector. She'd let him go then and sat silently until they'd reached the resort hospital.

CHAPTER TWO

'I THINK YOU may have sufficiently embarrassed the barman, Lollipop.'

Amy's face broke out into an uncontrollable grin and she turned back to where the voice behind her was coming from.

'Don't call me that.'

'What's wrong, Lollipop?' He smiled. The slow, lazy smile that he specialised in. 'Lost your sense of humour?'

'No…' Amy grinned. 'But I *have* lost my tolerance for your teasing. And if you haven't noticed…' Amy put one hand on a hip and pushed it out '…I'm not as skinny as I used to be.'

Yeah, he'd noticed. Luke beat down the heat pumping through his veins. Amy wasn't the skinny teenager of eight years ago. She'd changed. Filled out. His eyes slipped to her chest. *Really* filled out. And although he'd always considered her a pretty girl, she'd always been just that—a girl. But she wasn't a girl any more. She was a woman. And, by the looks of the body she was showing off in a tight white skirt and tan silky blouse, she was *all* woman.

But she was still his little sister's friend. Her silly, irresponsible friend. The girl who was too pretty for her own good. The girl who made an art form out of flirting. And that hadn't changed. The barman was still flushing and throwing furtive glances Amy's way.

'Some things have changed, but not everything.'

He nodded towards the barman and Amy turned to see the direction of his gaze. The barman smiled shyly before fumbling with a glass and allowing it to drop with a loud smash to the ground.

He leaned in close to Amy's ear so no one else could hear. 'Still making men do stupid things.'

As soon as the words had left his mouth he regretted them. He watched her stiffen. He felt her shrink away from him and her cheeks burned an instant red. He hadn't meant *that*. Not what she thought.

'Amy, I...'

She smiled. Wide. Fake. 'It's okay.' She gathered drinks. She hoisted her purse under her arm, flicked her hair and left. Making him feel like the most insensitive man in the country.

He knew what had happened all those years ago wasn't her fault. She'd been a kid. Sure, she'd been silly, naïve—reckless, even. But who wasn't at that age? She hadn't deserve what had happened to her and he'd made sure that the loser who'd attacked her understood how wrong he'd been.

Luke watched her walk back to the table filled

with people he hadn't seen in years. People who had once been closer to him than his family. People who'd made him feel normal. People who'd made him feel as if he belonged somewhere for the first time in his life. For the *only* time in his life. He'd never felt like that since.

The memory of that summer on Weeping Reef had got him through some tough times in his life. Had it only been a few months they'd all lived together on the island? It had seemed like longer. It had seemed that summer had lasted for years. It was the place where he'd remembered being young. Having fun. Being himself. But that was over. His reality now was work and responsibility and money and more work.

And he liked his life. He didn't want to go back. He'd grown up so much since then, learned so much. He was different now. Stronger.

But as he watched Amy walk away, clearly angry and upset, he didn't feel strong. He felt twenty-four again. Inept. Out of his depth and totally unable to decide what to do next. At twenty-four he would have ignored it. Ignored *her*. Ignored the way she felt and the fact that he'd put his foot into it. He would have sat with the others and said nothing. Carried on as if nothing had happened.

But he wasn't twenty-four any more. He was turning thirty-two in a month. And over the years he'd learned that the only way to solve a problem was to throw himself into it. Avoiding problems always made them bigger, more bad and harder to solve. Walking away was for sheep, and he wasn't a sheep. Not any more.

His feet flew across the floor and he had his arm on hers before she even sat down. 'Amy, I'm sorry. I didn't mean that the way it came out.'

Her eyes shot up to his. The same pretty brown eyes he remembered from all those years ago, but now a little more lined around the edges. From laughing. Or perhaps from crying. Probably both. If her life had been anything like his it would have been filled with both over the last eight years.

There were no tears in her eyes now, but there was something else. A fierce, angry determination he'd never seen before.

'It doesn't matter, Luke, that was a long time ago.'

She turned away, but he wasn't letting her go. She didn't fool him. There was no way she didn't still think about what had happened. He did. A lot.

During the last year in particular he had thought about it constantly. Since Koko. Since he had almost been the father of a daughter himself. He'd thought about all the things that could go wrong. All the trouble a girl could get into. He'd braced himself. He'd been as prepared as he could. He'd actually been looking forward to it after the initial shock had worn off.

'Amy.' He took the drinks from her hands and placed them on the table before moving a little closer to her. 'I'm sorry.' He held her eyes. 'I meant you're still an impossible flirt.'

'Is that what you think of me?' Her eyes hardened. 'I'm just a silly flirt who deserves everything she gets?'

She hissed the words and as he held her arm he could feel her shake just a little. Clearly it wasn't okay. Clearly she still thought about what had happened all those years ago. And clearly he'd put his foot in it big-time.

Her eyes darted from one of his to the other. Challenging. Hard. No fear, just distrust. That made his gut clamp hard. He didn't want her to feel that way about him. For some reason that was important. He didn't want her to feel she couldn't rely on him.

'No, Amy. That's not what I think. I like how you flirt with everyone you meet. You're friendly and sweet…if a little naïve. But I like that about you. I always did.'

He didn't move his hand from her arm or his eyes from hers. He couldn't let her go. Not until she realised that he had her. He wasn't going to hurt her. Something inside him burned to let her know that.

'I was just teasing you.'

She stayed silent but didn't move. The noise of the bar whooped around them but right then Luke couldn't concentrate on anything but her and his need to make her understand what he meant.

'What happened to your freckles, Lollipop?'

Her brow furrowed and her eyes lost that angry gaze. 'What?'

'Your freckles…across your nose.' He softly grazed the top of her nose with the tip of his finger. 'They've disappeared.'

A smile involuntarily moved his mouth. That summer they'd spent most of their time in the sun. Amy had worked on Reception but she had often gone out 'delivering a message' or 'taking a parcel'. He'd known what she was up to. She'd skipped out as much as possible to enjoy the sun and find his sister to get into mischief.

As the resort manager he should have hauled her into his office, gave her a warning—told her off, at least. But Amy had had a way about her. Cute, cheeky, sweet with just a whiff of sexy. He'd never been able to do anything more than give her slap on the wrist. And she known it. And she'd taken advantage of it. Batting her eyelashes and flashing her magnetic smile whenever she wanted something.

His eyes moved from her nose to her eyes. They weren't batting their lashes at him now. They were still. And hot. He saw something. Something that hadn't been there eight years ago. A sudden curious hunger that he knew he was transmitting right back to her.

No, no, *no*. This wasn't right. He stepped back a little, letting go of her arm. He couldn't feel *that*. Not with *Amy*. Not with little, scrawny, troublemaking Amy. His sister's best friend. His *little* sister's best friend.

But she wasn't that little any more. She didn't seem young at all. She looked… His eyes landed on her lips. Full and soft, they were covered in hot pink lipstick. She looked…*delicious*. His tongue darted out to wet his own bottom lip. Everything in his body

stirred. She was right—she was no lollipop any more.
The pretty little nymph had blossomed into a gorgeous woman, and she was looking at him now as if
she was thinking exactly what he was. *Sin.*

'There are a lot of things about me that have
changed, Luke.' Her voice had changed. It was deeper,
with a hint of husk. 'And one of them is that now I
know when to flirt harmlessly…' She moved closer,
her breasts brushing his arm. He looked down and
watched them—tanned and bouncing slightly as she
moved. 'And when to flirt with intent.'

'And what are you doing right now?'

'Oh, I think you know *exactly* what I'm doing.'

His eyes moved up quickly and checked hers.
'Well, I hope you know what *you're* doing. You don't
want to find yourself in more trouble than you can
handle.'

She moved even closer and the stirring in his body
started to roar. Quietly, slowly, but persistently. This
wasn't little lollipop Amy any more. This was a
woman well aware of her power.

'You think I can't handle you, Luke?'

Luke's mouth dried up. The idea of her handling
him was doing violent things to his body. Things were
springing to life. He had to calm this down.

'I think you might have enough to handle with all
the booze being passed around this table.' He nodded towards the table full of glasses. Some shots of
tequila had arrived and were being scattered amongst
the others.

She looked away quickly, then back at him. Hard. Hot. He held steady.

'Not scared, are you, Luke?'

'Scared? Of what?'

She smiled. A magnetic bright white that glowed in the dark bar. She shrugged a little. 'You tell me.'

Luke's heart beat steady but hard. She'd pegged him. He *was* scared. Scared that he actually wanted to take little lollipop Amy home, get her naked and kiss her entire body. And that he'd enjoy it. And he'd want to do it again and again.

But he wasn't going to do that. Not with her. She was too close. She wasn't someone he wanted to hurt. And hurt her he would, if he let himself go there.

'The only thing I'm scared of is that this lot are going to get kicked out if they get any drunker.'

He looked behind him at the group of old friends. Laughing so hard they were falling off their stools. Passing shots of tequila around, talking louder. and getting more animated with every drink. *Fun.* That was what they were. Fun, easy and carefree. And Luke wanted a little bit of that. He'd just gone through the toughest year of his life and he was back here in Sydney for this. Fun. Not Amy. Not relationships. Tequila. Laughs. Old friends.

He swiped two shots off the table and handed one to Amy.

'We may as well join them, Lollipop.' He swept the liquid into his mouth and enjoyed the burn as it travelled down his throat. Get drunk. That was what he was going to do tonight. Then he'd be able to forget and relax and maybe live a little.

What he *wasn't* going to do was his little sister's best friend. He planned on staying right away from *that* little wasps' nest, because he sure wasn't ready to get stung again.

CHAPTER THREE

THE HOT TEQUILA warmed Amy's already hot blood. She watched Luke as he necked another shot. What the hell was she *doing*? Flirting was something she did. With everyone she met. She'd always done it. She'd realised from a young age that she often got what she wanted with a little bit of sugar rather than salt.

From a young age she'd also realised that her flirting could sometimes land her in trouble, so she'd taken great care to tone it down in the past eight years. She only flirted outrageously with people she knew well—like Dave the barman, who happened to be one of her little brother's mates. But she shouldn't have flirted so outrageously with Luke. Could she make it any more obvious how she felt about him?

Amy sidled in next to Willa on the red velvet banquette. More partygoers had arrived and the room was filling with hot bodies. Inside her chest the usual thrill of excitement thumped. But tonight there was something else in there. Caution. An unmissable beat.

Calm the hell down. But it was hard to tell her

heart to do that with Luke sitting right opposite her, with his big hard body and his come-to-bed eyes that had just locked with hers so hard she'd thought she'd never prise them loose.

'What the hell happened? That was a pretty heated conversation.'

Amy glanced at Luke as Willa spoke. A couple of vodka sodas and her friend's whispering hiss echoed like a train in the desert.

'Shh.' Amy moved a little closer so she could hiss herself into Willa's ear. 'Your brother hasn't changed at all. He still thinks you and I are two little girls who can't take care of ourselves.'

'What did he say?'

He'd said she was still making men do stupid things. As soon as he'd said it she been able to tell he regretted it. She knew he hadn't meant it as it had come out. She couldn't remember how many times he'd told her over and over that night that it wasn't her fault. That just because she'd been friendly it hadn't given that loser the right to expect anything from her or to do…what he did.

Amy pushed down the swooping, then glanced at Luke. His eyes met hers and her stomach settled. He hadn't meant that. He'd rushed straight over to her to tell her he hadn't meant that. But what if he was right? Maybe she *was* flirting a little too fiercely. Amy hitched at her shirt. Maybe she was exposing too much skin.

No. No! Stop! she scolded herself. What had happened hadn't been her fault. The way she dressed and the way she spoke to people had nothing to do with what had happened. It had been *his* fault. This shouldn't ever have been her problem, her hang-up.

Amy shook herself physically. When she'd come home from Weeping Reef her mother and father and even her little brother had wrapped her up in their little cocoon of a family and helped her recover. That was when she'd met Laurie. Sweet, nice Laurie. Who'd loved her. Who'd made her feel whole again.

She'd hadn't thought about what had happened in years. It had only been in the last six months, since her old friends from Weeping Reef had come back into her life and their stories had been rehashed, that she'd thought about it again. But she was strong. She was tough. She wasn't going to let the memories of one bad night make her into a victim.

'Ames? Was he awful?'

'No, not at all.' Amy shook her head and turned back to her friend. 'Sometimes I'm just too sensitive. And besides, I think I'm still in a little bit of shock that he's even here. You should have warned me!'

'I'm sorry about that, Ames. It happened so suddenly. And anyway, there's no need to be embarrassed. You had a crush on him years ago. He probably doesn't even remember anything about it... or...anything else. And he wouldn't even care. You know Luke—keep the peace, stay cool, never let anyone know what you think.'

'Yeah...'

That *had* been Luke eight years ago. She'd fallen over herself back then to get him to notice her. That night with that horrible guest had been all about trying to make Luke jealous. She'd been trying for months to get him to notice her but he hadn't. All Luke had wanted to do was work and haul her into his office to tell her off every time she bent a staple.

The old Luke would never have apologised. The old Luke would have said nothing. He'd have let her walk away. She knew his theory—*not my monkeys, not my circus.*

But tonight he hadn't let her walk away. He was different. He *looked* different. Older. Harder. Stronger. Sexier. Amy bit her bottom lip as she sneaked another glance at him. That same strong jaw—only now wider. That same thick dark hair—shorter, but still with a hint of wave. His skin wasn't as tanned, and he'd put on weight, but she could tell that underneath that suit he was all muscle.

He had taken off his jacket now and was laughing at something Brodie said as he rolled up his sleeves. His large forearms strained against the fabric and heat settled in Amy's core. Her skin tingled. Even after eight years she still found him attractive. She still wanted him more than any other man she'd ever wanted. Even Laurie.

A flush of heat passed across Amy's forehead and am ache rushed to the back of her neck. She'd never forgotten Laurie's tears at the airport when she'd left Melbourne. But she'd had to go. She hadn't been in love with him any more. She'd known she was breaking his heart by leaving, but she hadn't been able to keep on lying and saying everything was fine. She hadn't wanted to be with him any more. She'd been healed. She'd needed to move on.

But now, as she looked at Luke, she wondered if she really had.

The night wore on, as many of their nights together did. Full of laughter and stories that started with, 'Do you remember that one time…?'

Normally Amy would be at the centre. Her stories the loudest and most animated, with just a hint of exaggeration to make everyone laugh. But tonight Luke's presence made her retreat a little. She worried about what he thought. She couldn't help it. Even after all this time and eight birthdays she still wanted him to like her.

'So what else have you been up to, Amy? Besides work? Cause that's all you seem to do, according to these guys.'

Luke was looking much more relaxed after an hour of so of drinking and swapping insults with Scott and Brodie. He'd edged closer to her, so now his knee was just inches from hers.

Amy was feeling the effects of the tequila and the vodka. She'd relaxed and was enjoying taking a back seat for once. Instead of being the one who was always up and down getting drinks, or moving between conversations, she was sitting back and enjoying watching her friends have fun.

'Having fun. Keeping this lot entertained. You know what it's like—there's always a party to go to or someone wanting a piece of you.'

Amy smiled. She loved her life. She loved being busy, and having a big circle of friends was important to her. At first coming to Sydney had been hard. She'd been used to being part of a big group of family and friends in Melbourne and she'd found herself all alone. That was until she'd moved in with Jess and started to go out—and then, when she'd run into Willa by chance one night in a restaurant restroom, her social life had become manic.

Catching up with the guys from Weeping Reef was almost a full-time job—they'd all aged, and their relationships had definitely changed, but one thing hadn't. This group loved to party.

'I know what that's like. It isn't easy, being pulled in a dozen different directions. Do you miss home? How are your parents? And your brother—Antony? Does he still have all his animals?'

Amy's brow furrowed and she leaned back a little. 'You remember my brother?'

Luke had never met Antony. She hadn't remembered ever telling Luke about him, and even if she had it was impressive that he could remember after all that time.

'Sure. You told me about his obsession with saving animals. I remember you saying that every time he came home from school he had another injured animal in his backpack.'

Amy laughed. That was her little brother. When they were young their family home had always housed at least a dozen animals Antony had rescued and nursed back to health.

'He's a vet now—which was no surprise to anyone. At least that means the animals stay at the clinic and don't come home. Although I was talking to Mum the other night and she said Antony had lobbed up with a wallaby for her to feed while he went away for the weekend.'

Luke smiled and his eyes crinkled. Amy watched it. She watched the way his mouth broke out into that smile.

'So you still talk to your parents a lot?'

'Not as much as I'd like.' Amy stared into her half-full drink. 'I miss them. They're crazy and loud, and Mum is always trying to force me to try some new recipe that contains the latest "superfood", or get me to drink things like chlorophyll and whatever else she's read on the internet. But they're…you know… home.'

'Home.'

Amy met Luke's eyes and they were locked on her. She'd felt him watching her for most of the night. As if he wanted to keep her in his sights. He was probably afraid she was going to do something stupid again, as she'd had a habit of doing when she was eighteen.

'Where's home for *you* these days, Luke? Willa tells me you're some millionaire, swanning around on yachts with a different gorgeous woman on your arm every night. A hotel magnate, or something.'

Luke let out a whisper of a laugh. 'Willa makes it sound much more fun than it is. Home for me is wherever work is. It's been Singapore for the last two years. I started a new development there and I've been trying to get it off the ground. The Singaporean government are usually easy to deal with when it comes to western investment, but for some reason they dragged their tails with this one…' Luke smiled and looked away. 'But you don't want hear about that.'

He straightened his spine and rested his hand on his knee. Amy watched as his fingers spread. Long, thick fingers. The alcohol was clearly taking hold, because all she wanted to do was reach out and lace her fingers through his. Feel the warmth of his skin.

Really bad idea, Amy scolded herself. *Not Luke.*

Amy had met a few hot men in Sydney to relieve the pressure, but she'd found it difficult to meet someone she was interested in dating. She'd found it difficult ever since Laurie, really. The men she met seemed interested in her looks and where she lived, but she hadn't actually met anyone interested in *her*.

'Sure I do. My new account is with a hotel chain, so I'd love to hear about your work, actually. I have absolutely no idea about the industry, so I'll be hanging off your every word hoping you let some juicy PR secret out.'

Truth was, she liked to listen to him talk. He was one of those rare men who actually had something to say.

'Feel free to drop in to my office here in Sydney any time and talk to my PR. Tonight I don't want to talk shop, though. I just want to get drunk and relax.'

The booze *had* relaxed him, but for the first time Amy noticed the dark circles under his eyes. He ran a hand absently thought his hair. He looked tired and worn. Something he'd never looked eight years ago. Weeping Reef had been his first proper management job and back then he'd taken it very seriously. You didn't step out of line when Luke was in charge or you were out.

'Hard day at the office, dear?' Amy teased, and Luke glanced her way with a smile.

'Hard few years, more like it.'

'So does that mean your home is here now…for a while?'

Amy didn't want to sound anxious, but she was. Although she knew she could never be with Luke the way she wanted, the idea of him being close was strangely comforting.

'For a while.'

He smiled directly at her. That killer smile he'd used on the island when things had been going well.

'Good.'

'Why's that good?' His green eyes darkened.

Amy couldn't help it. She shifted forward till their knees touched. She just wanted him to *know*. She wasn't sure if it was the tequila or loneliness or nostalgia, but she wanted Luke to know that she was glad he was staying and that her foolish girlish heart still found him hotter than a car bonnet on a summer's day.

'It's good because it might be nice having you around. I've kind of missed having you tell me what to do, and criticising my work, and the way you used to say, "Not *again*, Lollipop."'

He laughed out loud when she lowered her voice to mimic the way he spoke.

'I did used to say that a lot, didn't I?'

'At least once a day. You were a horrible boss.'

'I was a very tolerant boss, if I remember, and *you* were a terrible receptionist.'

'I was the resort's greatest asset.'

'You certainly knew how to keep the guests entertained.'

Amy stilled.

'Don't go getting all offended again, Lolli. You know I didn't mean it like that. What I meant was that our rebooking rate was one hundred per cent because of you and the way you kept in touch with every guest—emailing them about special deals and sending them postcards saying we all missed them on the island. Those ideas were marketing genius. If you'd put that much effort into filing your paperwork maybe you wouldn't have had to spend so much time in my office.'

Amy laughed. 'Maybe I stuffed up the filing because I *wanted* to spend more time in your office.'

She winked and Luke's brow furrowed.

'What…?'

'You know…'

'Know what?'

'About my mad crush on you.'

'Yeah, right. I think you may have had a mad crush on just about *everyone* back then.'

'Maybe. But you were my maddest. And don't say you didn't know. I practically threw myself at you.

How about the way I used to wear my shirts unbuttoned almost to my belly button?'

'Yeah, you did. I was forever telling you to dress yourself properly.'

'And all those after-hours bar dances. They never happened when you weren't there.'

'Sure they did.'

'No. They didn't. I could tell you about a hundred times when I embarrassed myself, trying to get you to notice me—but you never did, did you?'

'Sure I did. I noticed. I noticed an extremely pretty girl who had a lot of growing up to do.'

'Well, I'm all grown-up now.'

'Yes, you are.'

They sat like that for minutes—too many minutes.

Then Chantal and Brodie called from the other end of the table. They were leaving. Amy pulled her eyes from Luke's and checked her phone. Midnight. She had to go into work tomorrow—she really should think about going home too. But something about Luke made her want to stay. She wanted to be close to him, to be near him. He made her feel…something she hadn't felt in a long time. Something comfortable and warm and exciting all at the same time.

'We're moving on, Ames—you coming?'

Willa stood to leave. She and Rob and the others would probably end up at Milly's—the nightclub around the corner where they often partied until daylight.

'Not tonight, Wills. I have to get up and work tomorrow. I think I might have to call it a night.'

'What?' Jess was very drunk. Her hair had come loose and she'd spent the last ten minutes hugging everyone in the bar goodbye. '*No!* Come on, McCarthy—we're going out!'

'No—no, I'm not.'

Those words were hard to say, and they tasted strange coming out of her mouth. But she had to say them. Despite wanting to kick the party on with Jess, and despite the irresistible pull towards Luke. She was a grown-up now. Her bosses really were expecting her to nail this account, and she really couldn't let them down. She had to leave.

'You can't go home alone, Ames…'

'I'm a big girl, Willa.'

'I know, but you really shouldn't travel by yourself.'

Amy rolled her eyes. She'd managed to get herself around Sydney every day and night for the last nine months, but Willa still worried about her. It was sweet, but unnecessary.

'She won't be travelling by herself. I'll take her home.'

Amy's head whipped round at the sound of Luke's deep voice.

'No, Luke. You don't have to do that…'

'Yes. I do. If you think I'm letting you find your own way home at midnight in the city then you're drunker than I thought.'

Amy wasn't drunk at all. Not by her usual standards, anyway. She was sober enough to realise that having Luke take her home was safer than going alone. But she was also sober enough to realise that she was drunk enough to maybe throw herself at him, given half the chance. And she didn't want to do that.

And then he stood and rose up before her like a Viking, all tall and strong and broad...

Where had *that* association come from? Maybe she was drunker than she'd thought. She let her eyes drop and they rested right on him. On the part of his body she was most curious about. Slowly she licked her lips. She'd fantasised so many times about sex with Luke. Would he be gentle and accommodating? Or would he throw her against the wall, make her shut up and have his dirty way with her? She couldn't decide which one she wanted first, but she suspected that she wanted to try them all.

Slowly Amy's gaze rose to meet his eyes. 'I don't need a chaperon any more, Luke, I've managed to take care of myself quite well over the past eight years.'

'Well, maybe I do.'

Amy stilled. What did *that* mean? Luke hadn't left her side all night, and she'd noticed him looking at her. She wasn't an idiot. She knew there was something there. An attraction. The old Luke would have ignored it, but the new Luke seemed a little different. A little more aware of his feelings and more prepared to deal with them. She wondered what he'd do with his feelings for her...

Ten seconds later she had her answer. 'Get your coat, Amy—we're going home. Together.'

It didn't take long to find a taxi. The night was hot,

and people were careening noisily down the laneways of the inner city suburb, but the taxis were out in full force, picking up the Friday night revellers as they moved from bar to club.

Amy slipped into the seat and Luke followed, sitting a little too close, pressing his big leg up against hers.

The ride to Amy's flat in Bondi was silent, but the air was filled with tension. Every movement, every sigh, every look put Amy on alert. The buildings sped past on the main roads, but as they got closer to the beachside suburb the taxi slowed down to navigate the twisty turns of the narrow streets and the plethora of speed bumps that littered the way.

Luke wasn't looking at her, but his leg was still pressed up against hers. She felt it, hard and definite. The rocking of the taxi was lulling her and letting the alcohol settle in her blood. She felt content. Safe. Safer than she had in months. Ever since she'd left Melbourne and Laurie.

But sitting in the taxi with Luke was nothing like sitting with Laurie. Not even in the beginning. She and Laurie had met through their parents, and he had been just what she'd needed at the time. He'd adored her. He'd thought she was the most beautiful, wonderful person ever to grace the earth and had expressed to her constantly how lucky he was.

He'd soothed her soul. He'd brought back her happiness. And she was grateful to him. But one day she'd realised she just wasn't in love with him any more. And she'd wanted out.

Laurie had bent over backwards, trying to get her to change her mind. And she'd tried to stay with him—she really had. She'd tried to convince herself that it was just a rough patch.

But one night she'd gone out with some workmates and kissed someone else and it had been then that she'd realised staying wasn't fair on either of them.

So she'd left—decided on a fresh start in Sydney.

Her parents had been upset. His parents had been angry. Laurie had called every day for the first three months. Amy had wanted to relent. She'd spent three months crying and talking and trying to explain why she'd needed to do what she had but they hadn't listened.

It had made being in Sydney even harder. She'd felt deserted. Judged. And all she'd been trying to do was be happy. But the people in her life who claimed to care her the most had seemed to want the opposite of that. They'd wanted her to settle. Be happy with what she had because it made *them* happy.

The only thing that had got her through was Jess and Willa and her work. Her parents had come round eventually too, but she still had to stay busy and high—otherwise she'd be reminded of how she'd let everyone down, and then all she'd want to do was go back home and make it up to them. Go back and make everyone happy.

'You're quiet, Amy. You're never quiet. What's wrong?'

Luke's voice broke gently into the silence.

'Nothing. Just tired, I guess.' She *was* tired. Tired

of always trying not to think about the things that made her unhappy.

'I'm tired too. So much for me being a massive party animal tonight.'

He smiled and shoved his shoulder gently into hers. She shoved him back and he shoved her again. Their gentle shoves soon turned into pushing, and finally a little wrestling.

Luke grabbed at the back of her head. 'You always did think you were tough, Lollipop, but I know you're not.'

Amy pushed Luke's hand away. 'I'm tougher than you think, Boss.'

Luke smiled, 'You haven't called me that in a long time. I think I like it.'

The wrestling stopped. The air in the taxi turned a little thick. Amy stopped moving and stilled her hand where in rested, on his thigh. High on his thigh. *His* hand stilled on her head.

'You like it when I call you Boss?'

Amy's eyes skated to Luke's lips. They were slightly parted. She wanted to kiss him. She wanted to touch him. She wanted to do bad, bad things to him.

'I like having your hand there.' Luke's voice was deep, and he shifted his leg a little where her hand sat.

There was no mistaking what he wanted and how he felt. It sent a thrilling ripple through her to think that she could finally have what she'd wanted all those years ago. Time alone with Luke. Luke wanting her. It was everything she'd wanted as an eighteen-year-old and she could finally take it—if she wanted.

Carefully she shifted a little closer, her eyes still on his lips, her hand inching further up his thigh.

'Like this?'

A deep, low growl escaped from Luke's lips and Amy felt herself heat from the sound of it. *This was it.*

Quickly she pulled her hand away. 'You wish,' she said lightly, trying to clear the fog in her brain and the memory of his green eyes on her as she moved her hand up his leg.

Luke didn't answer. She couldn't tell if he was angry or embarrassed.

But then his hand moved and settled on her thigh. 'Good move, Lollipop,' he said quietly as the taxi finally came to a stop.

The heat of his hand on her thigh seared through her clothing. Why had she chosen that night to become responsible and sensible? She didn't *want* to be sensible. She wanted to be eighteen and reckless and to throw herself on Luke right here in the back seat of the taxi.

But she knew she couldn't. Because there was no way it would be a one-night thing with Luke and she couldn't offer him any more than that. She wasn't ready for another relationship. She didn't want to get involved in anyone's life. She still hadn't dealt with the fallout of her last failed relationship—she sure as hell wasn't about to throw herself into another mess.

She also knew that if Luke only wanted a one-night thing she'd be heartbroken. And, as she felt her body heat from her toes to her forehead at the mere touch of his hand on her leg, she knew in an instant that anything with Luke would get messy.

'Thanks for bringing me home, Luke. You didn't have to—but thanks anyway.'

'Any time, Lolli. I'm here for a few months now. I'll be around if you ever need me...for anything.'

Anything? Like hot sex?

'I should be all right. I've survived eight years without you so far.' Amy laughed, trying to keep it light. Trying to prevent him from seeing what she really wanted—for him to grab her, kiss her and insist on coming in.

But he didn't do that. He took his hand off her knee and opened the door to get out.

'No! No. Don't get out. I can walk to the front door.'

'I'm walking you to your front door, Amy.'

'No. You're not.'

She would punch him square in the face if she had to. She didn't want him walking her to the door, because she wasn't sure she wouldn't throw herself on him for a kiss goodnight, then force him to come upstairs and have his wicked way with her. No. A nice, chaste goodbye in the cab was the right thing to do.

But the kiss he landed on her cheek felt anything but chaste. It was soft at first, then he moved a little, closer to her lips and kissed her again, using his lips to soothe and caress her cheek. A kiss on the cheek—that was all it was—but Amy felt like melting right into him.

'Luke...' She wasn't sure what she wanted to say.

Don't. Stop. But those words wouldn't come out and the way she said his name sounded like a sigh.

'Amy.' He kissed her again, this time using his big hand to pull her cheek closer to him.

One touch. That was all she needed. To feel his skin one time. That would be enough.

Amy rested her hand back on his thigh and turned to face him. She kept her eyes on his—that way she'd know when he got too close and be able to pull away. But he didn't kiss her again. His mouth turned up a little at one side, but he kept his eyes on hers.

Amy's hand moved slowly but surely to his torso, and up further. She could feel the hardness of his stomach underneath her touch. She wanted skin. She needed to feel his warmth. So she tugged at his shirt till it was released from his waistband and enjoyed the relief coursing through her body as she hit his skin and continued moving upwards till she rested her hand on his chest. Hard and hot.

'That'll be twenty-four-fifty.'

The voice of the taxi driver broke the spell. Luke moved quickly, extracting the money from his wallet, practically throwing it at him, then flying out through the car door before Amy could protest. He was at her side and opening the door before she had time to breathe.

Stepping out into the night air should have felt better, should have cleared her head, but as the taxi sped away Luke stepped closer and she breathed in his scent again. Her head fogged. She turned into that silly besotted teenager all over again.

'Now how are you going to get home?' Her voice whispered it in the night.

'Maybe I won't go home.' His words were clear and gruff in her ear.

Amy moved closer as his arms encircled her waist. Maybe if she just felt his skin again she'd be done. She'd be able to move on.

'I like the feel of your skin.'

No. She wouldn't be done. His skin was hot and smooth, except for a sprinkling of hair on his stomach. She fingered it before moving her hands up and gripping his chest. She felt him tense and flex. This was more than flirting. This was dangerous territory. But with Luke it didn't feel dangerous. Exciting. Wrong. But not dangerous.

Luke breathed her in as he moved his hand over the silky blouse on Amy's back and gripped the back of her head gently. He needed her nearer. He moved her head closer to him. Dangerously close.

He needed to stop. But he wasn't going to. The alcohol, coupled with the relief of being home in Sydney and the surprise of seeing her again, had got under his skin. Everything was moving slowly. He could smell the prospect of sex in the air and he realised how much he wanted it. He needed it.

He curled his fingers through her hair. It was shorter now. Cut blunt to her shoulders. Nothing like the long, almost uncontrollable blonde hair she'd had back on the island. Back then her skin had been browner, her smile ready and willing. Here, she was different. Refined. Controlled. So unlike her.

He wanted to untie her, let her loose again. He wanted to see the carefree girl that he could still see in the flecks of gold that circled her brown eyes. But right now she wasn't carefree—she was serious. She was at her flirting best and he felt what those other men must have felt. The attention was intoxicating. The way she looked at him…as if he was the only man she'd ever looked at. The only man she'd ever felt this way about. Innocence and experience in one look.

'I like your lips,' he murmured to her.

They were still hot pink and full and slightly wet. He wanted to taste them. He wanted to taste *her*. Her hands massaged his chest. She wanted him too—he could feel that. And he wanted her.

He moved his other hand to her chest and touched lightly, circling her cleavage. Her eyes fluttered and she breathed more heavily. He watched every movement. He wanted to know how to turn her on. He let his hand cup her breast. He wanted to feel her underneath the silky shirt she had on. He wanted more of the soft warm skin he'd just been playing with. He wanted to touch all of her skin and kiss it, to bring out that wild girl he knew she had trapped inside. He wanted her to moan and squirm and scream and then he wanted to do it some more.

Amy's eyes met his. There was a heat in them he couldn't mistake. He knew what she wanted and there was no doubt she knew what he wanted. All he had to do was lean down, press his lips to her and drink her in.

This was Amy. Willa's little friend. The girl who got herself into more trouble than anyone he'd ever met. She never thought, so he should be doing the thinking for both of him. But his body wasn't listening. His body wanted her to move her hands down.

And as if she was telepathic, she did. Gently cupping him, then firmly wrapping her fingers around him through his pants.

He lost it. His mind stopped functioning. Logic and reasoning and everything he should possess left his body and all that was left was pure hot lust.

Swiftly, he took her lips. He pressed himself against her; let his hand fall to her chin so he could hold it steady. He wanted to keep her there till he'd finished what he was doing. His tongue moved against the seam of her lips and she let him in, shifting closer till those breasts were pushed right up against his arm. He shifted, letting her closer, and their mouths moved together. Slowly at first, but building up to such a frantic pace Luke was sure sweat was beginning to form on his forehead.

She was eager, pressing closer, and her hands were now on his back. It was just what he needed. Comfort and a warm body.

'Luke, you have no idea how long I've waited to do that,' she murmured, pausing only for a second and talking in a sleepy voice, her head tilted back so she could look at him before pushing herself closer and kissing him again—this time with force.

He wanted her. She smelled so good and tasted so sweet and her skin was soft beneath his fingers. But as soon as he heard those words he stopped. He couldn't do this. He *shouldn't* do this. She wasn't just a warm body. This was *Amy*. Little Amy. He couldn't let anything bad happen to her.

He'd let down enough women in his life. He wasn't going to do it again.

With a gentle push that spoke of finality he moved his head until she let go. Panting, she stared up at him, her eyes dark with lust, her lipstick almost kissed off and her perfect hair wild and falling softly over her left eye. Everything in his body went hard. She looked perfect. But he couldn't have her. That would be trouble, and the last thing he needed right now was more trouble.

'What's wrong?' she asked, moving her hands across his chest again.

It felt so good. Her hands were small but firm as they explored his muscles, making him feel bigger, stronger and better than he was. But he held her wrists and pulled them away.

'I'm not sure this is our smartest idea, Amy.'

She blinked as if coming out of a daze, then let out a breath. 'No. You're right. This is wrong.'

He didn't want to let her go but he had to. There were hundreds of thousands of eligible women in Sydney. He just needed to find one of them. Not Amy. Not her.

'This is a bad idea.'

'Very bad.'

She stepped back and wrapped her arms around herself. Right then she looked eighteen again. Innocent, unsure and wondering what she'd got herself into.

A memory of her sitting in that room flashed through his mind. Willa had called him. 'Amy's been attacked,' was all she'd said, and he'd flown to their villa.

Willa's eyes had been manic when he'd seen her and he remembered the way his stomach had sunk. He hadn't known what to expect, but when he'd opened the door to his bedroom he'd known he hadn't expected what he saw.

Amy had been sitting on her bed. Her wet hair plastered to her face with tears. Blood still fresh on her lip, her shirt torn and her bra exposed. She hadn't said anything. She'd just looked at him, then at Willa—clearly unhappy with him being there.

She'd been his responsibility. All the staff had. And for this to happen had burned his blood. But for some reason for it to have happened to sweet, carefree Amy had boiled him even more.

He'd kneeled before her. Asked her what had happened. She hadn't spoken. She'd just looked at him with tears rolling down her face. He'd held her eyes steady as Willa relayed the story.

It had been that slimy guest, Justin. He'd noticed them together. The jerk had been smooth. He'd been flirting with Amy all night, touching her. Luke had wanted to step in then, but he hadn't. He'd kept his opinions to himself. He'd known Amy was a bit reckless, but he hadn't thought she'd actually fall for the guy's lines.

He'd lost sight of them a little while later, when there'd been an emergency in the electricity room. They'd been gone when he'd come back. He should have checked on her. He should have made sure. But he hadn't. He'd gone back to his office to catch up on paperwork…

'I should go inside,' she said now.

'Yes, you should. And lock your door.'

'I will. Bye, Luke.'

'Bye, Amy.'

Amy gave him a strange look before walking up the path. He watched her punch in her security code. He waited till she'd climbed the stairs inside the glass door. He stood on the street till he saw a light go on at the second floor, where he assumed her apartment was. He waited for another twenty minutes on the street, watching another light go on, which he assumed was the bathroom—then all the lights went off.

And then, and only then, did he walk to the main road and flag down another taxi to take him home.

CHAPTER FOUR

THE FOOD AT THE waterfront hotel was good. The wine was chilled and the sun was beating down on their backs, but Amy's mood was still black.

'So what do you think it means?'

Willa was talking to her. She was saying something interesting and important, she was sure, but Amy couldn't remember a damn thing she'd said.

'I don't know, Will.'

'You're not even listening to me.'

'I am—I am.' Amy sat up straighter and looked her friend in the eye—or where her eye would have been behind the mirrored glasses she was wearing. 'You were saying about Rob and the flowers...'

'That was twenty minutes ago.'

Amy sucked in a deep breath. It was hot, and a headache was forming at the back of her head, and she knew exactly why.

She resisted the urge to check her phone. Again. Luke hadn't contacted her. It had a been a week. He knew where she lived—his sister was her best friend, for God's sake—he knew where to find her number but he hadn't. He hadn't called to check if she was okay after what had happened at her door and he hadn't called to catch up. Which he should have done.

'Right, Amy. Spill. I know you better than that. Something's up.'

Amy had told Willa that Luke had taken her home in a cab and left. She'd said he hadn't even got out. She didn't want to tell Willa the truth and that was churning her stomach as well. She told Willa everything. But the truth was she didn't even know how she felt yet, so she couldn't discuss it with Willa.

Luke was nothing. The kiss was nothing. So why did it feel like everything?

'I don't like it when you act strange, Ames. You're the only person who can make me get over myself and tell me the truth. And I need a hit of you. Where are you? Because you're not sitting here with me.'

Amy peered out past Willa's head to the water beyond. This wasn't like her. Amy didn't dwell. She got on with things—she moved on. Why the hell was she stuck on this? And on him. If he'd just call she was sure her brain would refocus and keep moving. She just needed to hear his voice.

'I'm sorry, Wills, it's this account at work. There's so much involved and so much to learn. I think my brain is a little frazzled by it all.'

'What you need is a night out.'

A night out. That was exactly what she needed. Cocktails. Cute boys and a killer dress. That would take her mind off Luke and her annoyingly persistent attraction to him and her ridiculous need to talk to him. She didn't need to talk to him—she'd not talked to him for eight years. A night out always fixed everything.

'You're right, Wills. A night out is exactly what I need—and I know exactly where to go. Our firm is representing Pete Middleton, who's just opened a hot new nightclub in the city. Envy, I think it's called. I'll get our names on the door for the VIP room. Call the girls.'

'Yay! Amy's back—I love it!' Willa clapped a little. 'But can our girls' night include a boy?'

'No. It's a girls' night. No boys allowed.'

'But I'm worried about Luke.'

Hearing his name froze something inside Amy. Willa wanted to invite the exact man she was avoiding? *No.* That wasn't the plan.

'Luke's a big boy, Willa—I'm sure he's fine.'

'He's been acting strange since he got back. Calling me a dozen times a day and asking me about Rob and if we're okay. He's never been that concerned before.'

'He was always over-protective.'

'Yeah, but he let me do my own thing. He always accepted my decisions. But he seems to be questioning everything at the moment. He wants to know Rob's background, and where he's from, and if he's making me happy. It's driving me crazy!'

That *was* a little strange. Luke had always been one to watch and keep an eye out for Willa, but he only ever stepped in if he needed to. And what made it even stranger was that he bloody wasn't calling *her*! Clearly he wasn't concerned about *her* welfare.

Heat crept all over Amy's body.

'Well, if he's so interfering, why do you want to invite him along? Wouldn't it be best to stay as far away from him as possible?'

Good advice. She should take it herself.

'I think he may be feeling a little lost and bored. I think he needs some distraction. Maybe if he does a few things he'll not be so concerned with me.'

'Maybe he needs a girlfriend.'

She was bitter. She knew that. But she couldn't help it. *He hadn't called!*

Willa's eyes softened and Amy knew what was coming. For some reason the two girls seemed to have a way of reading each other's thoughts, and right now Willa knew exactly what was going on.

'He didn't just leave in that cab the other night, did he, Amy?'

Amy remained silent. Anything she said could and would be used against her.

'Amy? What happened? Is there something going on between you two?'

Willa smiled, and Amy knew what she was thinking. Willa *wanted* something to happen between them. First, Willa knew the extent of Amy's crush on her brother all those years ago, and second, the idea of her best friend also being her sister-in-law would float Willa's boat.

Amy took a long sip of water. She was going to disappoint her friend. Not only was there nothing going on between her and Luke, she also knew there never could be.

It would be a nightmare if things went pear-shaped—which they would. It would risk her newly rekindled and much needed friendship with Willa, and Amy wasn't going to sacrifice that.

Amy knew that a random kiss with a stranger was all she could handle right now. Relationships were not on her to-do list. Not only was she still feeling guilty about the whole dumping Laurie and everyone hating her situation, she also wasn't sure if she'd be able to have a normal functioning relationship with anyone. Laurie had been Laurie. Kind, patient and accepting of her craziness—but would anyone else be so generous?

She wasn't sure, and nor did she want to find out.

'No, Wills. Don't get excited. The only person getting any action around here is you.'

'If you say so, Ames. If you say so.'

Amy could hear the smirk in her friend's voice but it was the truth—more or less. Disappointing though that was…

CHAPTER FIVE

Luke's name isn't on the door.

THE TEXT MESSAGE flashed on Amy's phone. *Damn.*
She'd thought Willa had gone off the idea of inviting
Luke. Clearly she hadn't, and now they were here and
she couldn't just turn him away. Although that was
exactly what she felt like doing. Particularly since the
jerk *still* hadn't called.

Amy avoided Luke's eyes when she met them at
the door. Instead, she spoke only to Willa.

'I thought you weren't bringing him.'

Amy knew she was being rude. Talking about
Luke while he was standing there. Tall, strong, and
with the fierce look on his face that had used to make
her melt. But she wouldn't melt this time. She was no
silly teenager any more. She was no one's slap and
tickle. *He should have called.*

'Trust me—I didn't want to come.'

Amy looked at his eyes then. What did *that* mean?
Did he regret the kiss? Did he not want to see her?
Well, two could play that game.

'No one's forcing you.'

'Fine. Good. I'll go. Call me when you need a lift home, Willa.'

'No!' Willa grabbed his arm as he made to turn. 'No, Luke. You're coming in and you're having a wonderful time.'

Luke didn't look happy but he stalked in—all darkness and clouds.

'Be nice!' Willa hissed to Amy as soon as he was out of earshot.

'I'm all rainbows and lollipops, Willa. It's your stupid brother who's got an attitude.'

'I know. He's had a bad day. But please try and be nice. For me.'

For Willa. Amy would do anything for Willa. And she wasn't exactly angry at Luke—just confused. What was wrong? Why was he being so damn rude?

The nightclub was clearly the current 'in' place to be in Sydney. Every B-grade celebrity had shown up, and Amy made her way around almost all of them. Her bosses would be even more in love with her when they found out about the publicity opportunities she was organising.

As the champagne flowed and the party bubbled along Amy managed to rack up event attendances, product endorsements, and even convinced a local TV presenter with massive boobs to bring her success-ful travel show to the hotel chain she was managing.

The night was going well, and Amy was getting what she needed—a temporary high. Except every time she glimpsed Luke her high left her. He wasn't looking at her, or talking to her, and every minute of neglect from him was making her blood burn.

'Amy McCarthy, your tits look amazing in that top!'

Matthew Davey. The biggest sleaze on the Sydney party circuit. He hit on everything that moved and had been pestering Amy for a date since she'd moved there.

'Matthew. You're...here.'

Normally Amy would turn on the charm. Matthew may be the biggest knob in the entire universe, but he had a super-successful health food supplement business and was currently in the market for a new PR agency. But there was something about Matthew that Amy didn't like. A certain way he'd look at her or accidentally touch her that made her skin crawl.

'Yes, I'm here. Have you been waiting for me?'

Amy didn't smile. 'Sure. Have you got a drink?'

His glass was full but she was more than happy to go away and find him another one. And then maybe 'accidentally' get lost on the way back.

'Yeah, I'm good, babe. Did you get my text the other day?'

She had.

The grassy knoll. One p.m. Saturday. Be there.

Amy had ignored it. Sitting amongst Sydney's most unbearable hipsters and putting up with Matthew on a hot, sticky afternoon sounded like her version of hell.

'Yeah, I couldn't make it—work, you know. It's hectic!' She raised her glass and sipped, looking away to see whose eye she could meet.

Where the hell was Willa? She'd get her out of this in the flick of an eyelash.

'You work too hard, babe. Listen—there's something I want to discuss with you. I've made my decision on who I'm going to go with for my account.'

'Mmm?' *Please not me, please not me.* Amy sipped her champagne again.

Matthew stepped closer. His aftershave wafted around her. It was a nice scent, but for some reason on him it just smelled cheap and nasty.

Matthew lifted a hand and gripped the upper part of Amy's arm. He was squeezing too tightly and it hurt. A searing heat ran through her. She schooled her breathing, turned her head to look at his hand, raised one eyebrow and looked him square in the face.

'Matthew, I don't know who you're going with for your account, and frankly I don't care. But if you don't take your hand off me you're going to wake up tomorrow with the blackest pair of balls known to man.'

'*Oooh!*' Matthew smiled, not removing his hand and moving in closer. 'Kinky. I like that.'

'What's going on here?' Luke's gruff voice broke into the space.

'What?' Matthew let go and snarled at Luke. 'Who are *you*?'

'Never mind who I am. I think it's time you left.'

'Why?' Matthew drew himself up. He was tall—

almost as tall as Luke—but nowhere near as thick-set. 'Go away, mate.'

Luke stepped deliberately in front of Amy, block-ing her view and meeting Matthew's eyes. 'I said, *leave.*'

'Okay, okay, okay...' Amy shoved herself in front of Luke. 'I think that's enough, Luke—everything's fine here.'

'You stay out of this, Amy.'

Luke's brutal, patronising words made Amy's body buzz. She understood what he was doing. She knew he was trying to help her. But she'd been helping her-self for these past eight years. The last time he saw her she might have been a pathetic teenager who made stupid mistakes and got herself into bad situations but that had been a long time ago. She'd learned to be more cautious. She'd learned to trust her instincts. She'd learned to stick up for herself and she didn't need him busting in, trying to be the hero.

'I *won't* stay out of this, Luke. I'm handling it.'

'It's all right, Amy, I've got this.'

He glanced at her and she saw the flash of green in his eyes. He was angry. But Matthew hadn't done anything really wrong. He was obnoxious and an-noying, but she'd already let him know his attentions weren't welcome.

'No, *I've* got this.' Amy turned to Matthew. 'Go away, Matthew.'

Matthew's eyes opened wide, as did his mouth. But he didn't say anything. He just threw Luke another dramatic look and left.

'You're lucky I was here.'

Amy turned back to Luke, her own face as shocked as Matthew's. 'Lucky? Why am I *lucky*? I had the situation under control.'

'You're not known for having situations under control, Amy.'

'*Excuse* me?'

'I was just trying to help.'

'No, you were trying to interfere. You stepped in without asking and just assumed I'm some idiot who can't control my own life.'

'That's not what I did, Amy. You were having trouble with that loser, so I stepped in before anything got any worse...'

'Oh, I *see*. You assume that I'm as stupid and naïve as I was eight years ago. That's it, isn't it? You don't see me as anything else but a silly eighteen-year-old and you never will. The same way you see Willa. Just a stupid little girl who made a bad choice and married the wrong man all because *you* weren't there to save her. That's why you're driving her crazy now. That's why you won't leave her alone. You're suffocating her, Luke, and she doesn't like it.'

Luke stared back at her, his eyes still flashing green. 'My sister is *my* responsibility. And, yes, I see Willa as someone I have to look after—but not because she's stupid and can't take care of herself. Because I let her down. I knew she shouldn't have married that man. I knew she was too young and he was too old for her. But I said nothing back then. Just like when—'

His eyes searched hers.

Was he talking about the night she'd been attacked? Amy flushed. She hadn't seen Luke again after that night. She'd shed a lot of tears over what had happened, but so many more over what Luke must have thought of her. And now she knew. He thought she was silly and naïve and couldn't take care of herself. The thought made her heart feel heavy—she didn't want him to think like that about her.

'There were times I let things happen that I shouldn't have, and that was wrong. So I'm sorry if you think that my coming over here and stepping in is interfering, Amy. I'm sorry if you think I shouldn't be the kind of man who steps in and takes action to stop the people I care about from getting hurt. But I *am* that man. I may not have been eight years ago— hell, I wasn't that man a year ago—but I am going to be that man now. I don't want to lose any more people in my life just because I sit around and wait for bad things to happen.'

Emotion rolled off him like a morning fog. His fists were clenched and he stood too close. His eyes glowed and Amy realised there was more going on with Luke than he was letting on.

He might think she was silly and always getting into trouble—he might not want her or even like her—but she knew when someone needed a friend, and from the look on Luke's face, she knew he needed one right now.

'Luke…' He'd turned to go, but Amy caught his arm. 'Luke, wait. Stop.'

He stopped and turned. 'What?'

Amy realised now why he was all up in Willa's grill. Because he needed to talk…about something that was bothering him. His speech about not being there for people when they needed him had been passionate and emotional, and that was so unlike him. Hard, cool and distant. That had been Luke eight years ago. Something had changed.

Eight years ago Luke had been there for her when she'd needed him. He'd been a friend in the most difficult time she'd ever experienced. And tonight Amy was going to return the favour.

'Do you still have that crazy sweet tooth of yours?'

Amy smiled and Luke's brow furrowed into two dents between his eyes.

'What?'

'Come with me, Boss. I'm going to take you to heaven.'

CHAPTER SIX

LUKE KNEW HE WAS probably sporting his orgasm face right now, but he couldn't help it. He was literally in heaven. Amy had taken him to a late-night bakery called Heaven and inside he'd found cakes, slices, ice cream, macaroons and every other sweet thing his boyhood dreams had been made of.

He avoided this type of food because he knew how much he loved it and would always eat too much of it, but tonight it was just what he needed.

He'd had a bad day. The Singaporean government had brought up more issues. His manager in Singapore had been able to take care of it, but it had irritated him. He'd come to Sydney for some much needed rest, but so far he'd done nothing but stress. About the Singapore project, about Willa, and now about Amy.

He'd been thinking about her since that night. He'd tried to stop but he couldn't. She was still that same girl he'd known all those years ago but something had changed. He couldn't put his finger on it. She'd always been confident, but it was different now. Not a reckless wild confidence in her looks and the way she could turn men on. Now her confidence seemed more internal. As if she'd actually learned to like herself instead of always wanting to feel that attention from others.

Sure, she was still a flirt, but she seemed more in control of it now and was somehow able to turn that confidence in herself into a generosity that had him captivated. Like tonight. Instead of staying angry, as she should have when he'd stepped in and interfered, she'd seen that he was upset and left the party to make him feel better.

Luke shifted a little closer to her. Somehow, in some crazy way, that made him feel even more protective of her. He wanted to protect that good, kind heart of hers and not let anyone hurt it.

'Good?'

Amy was smiling. Tonight she looked even better than she had before. With a slick of red on her lips that matched the fire-engine-red strapless top she had on, she looked polished and perfect. Professional with an incredibly sexy edge. He could see why she was perfect in PR. She was the ideal combination of warmth and smarts. If she hadn't already been kicking goals and clearly happy in her job he would have tried to poach her for himself.

'*So* good. You're going to make me fat, Amy.'

She laughed, and he was reminded of old Amy. That bright laugh had used to echo across the office constantly. She didn't laugh as much now, he noticed.

'You'd never get fat, Luke, you're way too disciplined for that.'

She was right about that. He made sure every hotel he built housed a well-equipped gym. Keeping his body under control was something he *could* do—and with his sweet tooth, it was necessary.

'How did you remember about my sweet tooth?'

She laughed again, and he found himself moving even closer to her on the curved bench they were perched on. He licked another piece of cake off his spoon.

'You always worked. You were always in your office, or scooting off on a golf cart to check on some problem. The only time you emerged and actually sat with us was on the days someone had a birthday and we got cake. Sometimes we made birthdays up just to lure you out.'

'No? You didn't!'

Amy laughed again. 'We did once. Remember we wanted new uniforms and you didn't have time to go through them and choose? We went and got your favourite cake—chocolate rocky road—and had all the uniforms out and ready for you.'

He didn't remember that. But he *did* remember not having enough time. He'd worked hard over the years on that, and now made sure he was across everything.

'You always were a ratbag, Lollipop.'

'And you always were hard to deal with.'

Amy lifted her spoon to her mouth and Luke watched as she poked out her tongue to lick it clean. Long strokes, getting every last piece of cake. His body hardened. He'd tried to stay away from her. He hadn't called or contacted her because he knew his attraction to her was wrong. And now he was reminded of why he should have stayed away tonight.

She dipped her spoon in for another piece. Her tongue came out before the spoon hit her lips and she closed her eyes as she sucked it. Luke put his cake down, his appetite gone. For food anyway.

'I'm not hard to deal with at all.'

Amy crossed her legs and her bare knee was now pointed at him. He wanted to touch her, just rest his hand there and feel that skin again.

'I'm a pussycat,' he said, trying to keep his voice level.

She laughed again and he smiled, right down deep inside. He liked it when she was happy. She deserved to be happy.

Amy placed her plate on the table but kept the spoon and absently licked it. He watched her tongue go in and out, wishing like hell that she was paying that type of attention to a part of his body that was now become uncomfortably large.

She leaned forward a little and her cleavage filled the red top. Swallowing, he lifted his eyes to hers. They were dark and warm, like the caramel fudge he'd just been eating.

'You're no pussycat…you're a big, unfriendly old lion. Even tonight you weren't happy to be here.'

'I've had a bad day. A bad week. I'm sorry.'

She sucked in a breath and her breasts moved up and down. Flicking her hair back, she leaned an elbow on her knee and rested her chin on it. Her dark eyes were big and she blinked at him. He licked his lips. Hot—it was so hot in here.

'And how about not calling me all week? Are you sorry for that?'

'Do you want me to be?'

'Luke, you don't kiss someone like that and then not call them.'

'I thought we'd agreed getting involved was a bad idea?'

'Did I say I wanted to get involved?'

'Well, what *do* you want, then?'

She moved closer, her face now level with is. Her scent met his nose and all his thoughts left his head. It was a week ago again, and this time he couldn't blame the booze. He wanted her.

'You. In my bed.'

'Be careful what you wish for.'

His blood pumped. He wanted this to happen. She wanted this to happen but knew it shouldn't. He *knew* that. But as her hand touched his leg he couldn't remember why.

'The thing is, Luke, I haven't had sex in a long time. A *very* long time. I find it hard to meet men I feel comfortable enough to want to get naked with. I know you think I'm a flirt and that I've probably got men tied up all over town...'

Luke had visions of her on top of him, his wrists tied and her doing whatever the hell she wanted. He put down his spoon.

'But I haven't. And the truth is I find you incred-

ibly sexy. And I want you. And I know this is a terrible idea, but—to be honest—I think you'd really be
helping me out.'

For the first time Luke realised Amy wasn't flirting with him. Her words were sincere. There was no
fancy flattery. She was matter-of-fact, and he found
himself liking it. She knew what she wanted. Sex.
With him. And he realised that it was exactly what
he wanted too.

She had the spoon in her mouth again, so he took
it, slipping it from her lips. 'I can help you out, Amy,
but you need to get rid of this damn spoon.'

In seconds, he'd replaced the spoon with his lips
and she drew herself closer, licking his tongue the
way she had been the spoon seconds ago. She tasted
like cake and he kissed her deeper, his arms circling
her small frame, dragging her to him. She responded
with a little moan which only made his body harder.

'We should leave,' she murmured, and he took no
time in getting her the hell out of there.

Amy's flat was only two blocks away but it seemed
too far. Every time she got more than two centime-
tres away from him he grabbed her, pulled her close
and started kissing her neck. She responded by turning and lifting her arms around his neck before kissing him back.

He wanted more of her—needed her horizontal.
She seemed to want the same, because she was pulling on him, pulling him down closer, her hands everywhere—on his back, behind his head, through his

hair. She gasped as she kissed him, barely coming up for air, and her desperation turned him on.

'If we keep kissing here we'll never get to your flat,' he whispered into her hair as she pulled him close again.

'I know, but I can't stop.' She pulled him again and he stumbled a little, accidentally pushing her so she stumbled too, but he caught her before she fell.

He laughed. 'Someone's going to get hurt.'

Grabbing at her from behind, he forced her to walk. But he didn't get far before the lure of the skin on the back of her neck called to him again.

This time she practically growled as she turned and jumped on him. Surprised, he stepped backwards, but found himself tripping on something. Before he could stop himself he was falling backwards into a bush in someone's garden, her right on top of him.

They clashed heads and landed in the leaves and Amy let out a little yelp.

'Are you okay?' he asked, holding her arms steady.

Strange noises came from her. At first he thought she was crying, and he struggled to get them upright, but she wasn't crying. She was laughing. It started as a giggle and ended in a contagious laugh with which Luke couldn't help but join in.

The bush rustled as they lay there, uncomfortable and sore, but unable to free themselves as they laughed heavily at nothing. She clung to him and he clung to her until their laughter subsided.

'You're just what I need, Amy.'

Her laughs evaporated and she looked at him. Her dark eyes were almost black in the night.

'Ouch,' she said, and moved to get up.

Not the reaction he was expecting, but possibly the best one she could give. This wasn't a relationship. This was just two friends helping each other out. He was glad she realised that, because they'd have more than a few scratches if they weren't on the same page.

'Help me up!' she whispered as the lights in the house were flicked on.

'Who's there? Is someone out there?'

They stilled, but the bush couldn't hold them, and then Amy shifted a little so that Luke had to adjust his position to hold her up.

'Who is it? I'm calling the police.'

With a struggle and a push Luke managed to get them both upright, and then he grabbed Amy's hand and pulled her hard. They ran off down the footpath, with abuse being hurled at them from behind.

CHAPTER SEVEN

AMY'S LUNGS BURNED. They'd run so fast, and she'd already been out of breath from all the kissing she'd been doing.

Kissing Luke was even better than she'd imagined it would be. He was confident and sure, and he'd held her so close and so hard she'd felt his desperation for her. It made her feel wanted and special. But she had to remind herself what this was about. *Sex.*

She'd decided to forget about Luke a few hours ago. But when he'd exposed himself to her with that speech about Willa being his responsibility and him wanting to be the kind of man who fixed things she hadn't been able to resist.

She wanted him all over again. Badly. And the truth was she hadn't felt that way about someone in a long time.

'Code?'

He was asking for her security code to get them into the building. He still had hold of her hand and it felt so good there.

'Zero, three, one, zero.'

He turned to face her. 'You shouldn't tell anyone your security code, Amy.'

Amy blinked. He was right. She *shouldn't* tell anyone her code. She would never normally tell anyone her code. But she'd blurted it out to him without any prompting. What was *wrong* with her?

'Don't worry, I'll have it changed by the morning. I don't want you breaking into my house while I'm not here and going through my underwear.'

His stern face disappeared and was replaced with a slow, sexy smile. He moved closer, slipping one hand down the front of her skirt to brush his fingers against the lace of her underwear. She sucked in a breath—a deep one. His fingers were confident and she wanted him to go further, explore deeper.

'How about I just do that out here?'

Deep and sexy, his voice made her legs shake.

'Open the damn door, Luke.'

He did—but not before he kissed her again, deeply, and with a force she'd never felt from Laurie. In comparison Laurie's kisses were soft, almost reverent. But there was nothing reverent about the way Luke was kissing her and moving his hand to get underneath the lace of her underwear.

Amy led the way up the stairs, pausing once to turn and kiss him again. She was finding it hard to go more than three seconds without feeling his lips on hers, and thankfully he responded the way she wanted him to. He stopped and kissed her back, his hands tangling in her hair as he pulled her face closer to him.

'Up, up...' he panted, and she moved backwards up the stairs before reaching the top and fumbling in her bag for the swipe card that would let her into her flat.

Before the door was even shut Luke had her up against the wall in her hallway. His hands worked on the zipper of her skirt as her hands fumbled with his buttons.

He was strong, and he held her as if she weighed nothing more than the packet of condoms she had in her bedroom—still unopened. Condoms she needed right now.

'My bedroom is down that way...' She struggled to get the words out as he kissed her lips, her eyes and her neck. That spot right between her collarbones. She'd never been kissed there, and she wasn't sure why it felt so damn good but it did.

The buttons undone, she finally got a look at the older, bigger, stronger and *tattooed* Luke. Across one side of his chest and down his shoulder were the black markings of a large tattoo. She couldn't make out what it was, and nor did she have time to look.

Luke was swiftly removing her top, pulling it up over her head, and he had her bra on the floor in seconds. His mouth moved down to her chest as he held her backside up against the wall. She ached to feel his tongue on her nipple. She wanted him to suck and lick and bite. She needed him right now, with a force she couldn't explain. This wasn't tender loving sex, like Laurie had offered, this was wild animal sex. And it was just what she needed.

'No time for bedrooms,' he said as he finally let her feet fall to the ground.

He moved down her body, his hands touching before his tongue licked. Her neck, her breasts, her nipples, her stomach… And finally he was pulling down her skirt and kissing the lace of her underwear. It was the only barrier between them now and she wanted it off. She tugged at it, trying to get it off.

The heat of his breath hit her bare skin as he helped her and she moaned loudly when he finally let his mouth kiss her swollen lips. She held his head steady as his tongue forced its way in. He licked with long strokes, and then with fast short ones. He moved his head a little to the side and kissed her, long and hard and deep, and Amy felt everything in her core shake.

She wanted to climb up onto his shoulders to get herself closer, but with a swift movement he already had her leg up. She pushed closer and he kissed deeper, delving with his tongue and sucking on her clit. Amy pressed closer. Laurie had never done it like this. *Never.*

She felt what Luke was feeling. He wanted her. Every bit of her. And he wasn't stopping until she was satisfied. But the orgasm wouldn't come. She clamped her stomach tight. She shifted away. She didn't want him to get sore, kneeling before her.

'Relax,' he murmured into her, which made a warm trickle flow up her spine. 'Relax, Amy. Let go. Enjoy it.'

His words murmured through her and she did what he said. She relaxed her muscles, she thought of nothing else but him and what he was doing, and within seconds the hot flash of a shaking orgasm tore through her. She bucked. She shook. It tingled up her body and then it was over.

Luke looked up at her, panting a little, his lips moist and his eyes greener than she'd ever seen them.

'Now we can move,' he said, a slow smile forming on his lips.

But she wasn't going anywhere. She pushed on his shoulders till he was on his back on the floor and then she tore at his belt. She had his pants down in seconds and hovered above him.

'Condom,' she said.

'Condom…' he repeated. But he didn't move.

Clearly he wasn't prepared—but she was. Quickly she sped into her room and fumbled through her drawer, trying to locate the pack she'd put there, intending to put it to use but not having done so yet. She slipped one from the packet and was back on top of him, ripping it open, in seconds.

But she was trembling too much to put it on. The orgasm was still freshly running through her body. So he took it from her hands and sheathed himself.

As soon as his hands hit the base she started. Slowly, purposefully sliding herself over him. A thrill ran over her as she lifted herself and then slid back down again. He was big, and she felt him throbbing inside her, but his face turned her on more than anything.

His mouth was almost a snarl and his eyes were focussed on her. Not her breasts, or her body, or what they were doing but connected right to her eyes—and she felt as if she could read his thoughts. His animalistic thoughts of just being in the moment and enjoying what she was doing to him.

His hands gripped her thighs and he moved her forwards, then backwards, faster and faster. She felt his gaze. It made her feel wilder, more free. She lifted her arms to her hair and let her mouth make the noises it wanted. She moaned, she sighed, she called his name.

He pushed her back and forth more frantically until he quietly growled, 'I'm going to come.'

She looked at him then—right into his eyes. 'I want you to come.'

And he did. Pulsating and pushing into her until another orgasm burst through her and shook her body. Abandoned, she shifted and moved until every last spark was spent, and then all she could do was fall on to his chest. Exhausted and dazed and much more satisfied than she'd felt in months.

CHAPTER EIGHT

THE SUN PIERCED Amy's eyeballs and she cursed loudly. She always remembered to pull the blinds before she went to sleep. *Always*. Because every morning the sun hit that spot that would fry her eyeballs and then sit there…just long enough to make sure she was awake and not able to go back to sleep.

She moved slowly, expecting her hangover to hit violently as soon as her head lifted from the pillow, but surprisingly her head felt okay. Was she hungover? No, of course not. She hadn't drunk that much last night. But she *was* hot.

She pulled the covers off, but just as they flicked to the other side she felt something she wasn't expecting. Warm flesh. Amy's head spun and everything returned in a rush. The nightclub…Heaven…falling in the bushes…the frantic backwards walk up the stairs and then the hallway…oh, the hallway.

Amy couldn't stop the smile that was spreading across her face. Because it hadn't been just the hallway. They'd made it as far as the lounge before they'd had to start kissing again, and then they hadn't even made the bed before he was on top of her and looking into her eyes again. Hard, direct and hot.

They'd laughed, and Amy had gone to get water, but by the time she'd returned he's been curled up in her bed. Naked and gorgeous. Which he still was now.

Amy wasn't sure whether it was the fact that it was Luke, but she'd never had sex like that before. Frantic and fast, desperate to taste, touch and be as close as possible to each other. He'd seemed to want her so badly, and it had made her want *him* even more badly. And as they'd kissed and touched and explored it had seemed nothing was off-limits. As if he was willing to do anything she wanted. And, God help her, last night she'd been willing to do anything to please him.

It was new. And dangerously addictive. But Amy had willpower. Loads of it. And she knew what this was. A reaction to a past life. Scratching an old itch. A way to pass the time while Luke was in town. It wasn't real and that was good. She didn't want real. She didn't want a relationship. Because relationships never lasted and someone always got hurt and she wasn't ready to do that again.

Luke moved. He rolled over, then opened one eye. He looked at her, and she smiled before giving him a little wave.

He opened his other eye and lifted his hand to wave back. 'Hi.'

'Hi.'

He lifted himself up with a yawn and a grunt and stretched. His thick torso shook as his fists rose up high over his head.

Amy bit her lip. *Willpower.*

'How are you feeling this morning?' he asked, his voice deep and sleepy.

Horny. 'Good. You?'

He met her eyes and paused before replying, 'Hungry, actually.'

'I have bread and… Actually, that's about it. Sorry.'

She and Jess didn't shop for groceries. They ate out. Toast and Vegemite was about all they had available in-house. And wine. There was always wine. But she guessed he didn't feel like wine.

'Bread?' He screwed up his face. 'That isn't going to cut it.'

'What do you want, then? This isn't a café I'm running, you know.' She mirrored his movements and propped herself up on one hand.

He smiled then—a lazy, slow smile—before bringing his big hand up to touch her thigh under the sheet. Amy shivered. Instantly her body overheated. Too many sheets covering her. She wanted to be completely naked. Exposed. And doing whatever he wanted. Hell, if he wanted to eat croissants off her stomach she'd let him.

Wait. No. Willpower.

'How about a bit of this?'

He grabbed a handful of her backside and roughly pulled her closer. Amy's nipples sprang to attention. Every hair on her body stood and her core started to throb. Slowly at first but then, as his hands moved and explored her skin, before coming round to rest right on her swollen folds, the throbbing beat overtime. She tried not to move. One move and his fingers would be inside her.

Willpower.

This visceral reaction was new. With Laurie it had taken foreplay and talking and a whole lot of negotiation. It had never been immediate like this. Laurie had never made her hairs stand on end. He'd loved her. Gently. Slowly. Respectfully. Laurie would have never grabbed her ass and pulled her so close she could feel him hard against her. She hadn't wanted him to.

But with Luke it seemed that clearly she did. Or her body did. It felt as if it was sparkling—as if it was alive for the first time in a long time—and she liked it. She didn't feel numb, for once, and she had Luke to thank for it. But that was all this was. Just an awakening. With a hot man she'd once had a thing for. Who she didn't have a thing for any more.

'A bit of what?' Amy teased, knowing what he wanted and wanting it too, but wanting to hear him beg. 'Don't you think you've had enough of that?'

'Not nearly enough.'

He snuggled in close and kissed her right behind the ear. Amy's back arched. A hot tingling streamed from the spot he was kissing right down to her toes.

'We should eat,' she protested, pulling away from him and meeting his eyes. They were almost blue. A sea-blue that reflected the ocean way offshore.

'I'm planning on it,' he growled, and kissed her long and hard on the lips.

Then, before she had time to breathe, he grabbed her by the waist and flipped her onto her back. She made all sorts of fake protesting noises but he cleverly ignored them. She squirmed a little, so he held her hips steady and sat up on his knees.

Amy admired the view. His chin was covered in a growth of twenty-four-hour stubble, his hair—although short—was standing in all directions. He looked a little beastly and a lot hungry. For *her*.

Amy had never felt so hot in her life. Normally she'd cover up, or make an excuse to calm things down so they wouldn't get out of control. So she could keep a handle on what was going on. But this was Luke. She'd known him for years. He knew her deepest darkest secret.

Her stomach swooped and he must have seen something flash in her eyes.

'Stop thinking. Just relax. Let me make you happy.'

He smiled and the swoop turned into something else. A more violent wave of sexual energy and excitement. The squirming to get away turned into a squirming to open her legs. Wider and wider, so his head could make its way down to where she was hot and swollen and oh, so wet…

'Delicious…' he murmured, using a finger to stroke her up and down before he pushed his way in.

Amy let out a guttural noise as Luke let his tongue explore, stroke and lick her. She shuddered happily. She tasted so good, and he loved being there in her warmth, feeling her buck against him. Her noises were becoming more frantic. She was close and he needed to slow it down. He wanted this orgasm to last a long time. He wanted her to really enjoy it and feel *everything*. But she tasted so damn good and was so responsive he couldn't let her go.

He tugged at her hips, bringing her down to his face.

He wanted to tell her to relax but he couldn't speak. Last night had been frantic and crazy, and when he'd woken this morning he'd wondered if it were all a dream. Then he'd seen her. Her blonde hair messed up, her eyes black from make-up and the sun belting in behind her, bathing her in some weird angelic light. Naked except for the sheet she'd held carelessly to cover her breasts. Then she'd waved, and a naughty look had crossed her face, and he'd been immediately hard all over again.

She was fun—he'd expected that. She loved sex. He hadn't expected that. He'd known she was flirty but he'd noticed a caution in her. Whenever a man spoke to her she wouldn't let him get too close. She often touched women when she talked, waved her hands about and lightly touched their arms when she laughed, but with men he'd noticed she was further away. Her voice was light, her laugh loud, but her body language was clear. *Don't get too close.*

Which was why, when they'd left Heaven, he'd been so surprised at her response. She'd leapt on him. She'd pushed herself into him, her lips hungry for the taste of him and her hands constantly moving over his skin. She'd made him feel bigger and stronger and so desired he'd lost his balance near that bush.

She'd ended up on top of him and he'd wanted to

wrap her in his arms and carry her home like some caveman. As if she were his. But she *wasn't* his. Not really. But right now she was—and right now it was his responsibility to give her the best damn orgasm of her life. And he was going to do it. She just needed to relax.

CHAPTER NINE

HE SHIFTED TO kiss her thighs gently, using the time to catch his breath and allow her to relax. She moaned and moved her hips. Her lips were swollen and open to him, and all he wanted to do was feast on her again, but he had to be patient. He wanted her to remember him.

He knew their time together wouldn't last long. It never did, and this in particular should never have started in the first place. But it had, so now he was determined that she'd remember him as the best damn sex of her life.

Swiftly he took her in his mouth again. He licked, then found the hard nub and sucked it gently while his tongue worked everywhere else. When she gripped the sheets tight and started to pant he knew she was close. Her hips rose up to his face…she pushed herself closer to him. *Wait. Wait. Not yet.*

Still he laved her, enjoying the feel of her on his lips and the way she was now gripping his hair, trying to get him closer, moving faster. *Now.* She was going to burst.

Luke gave her one last long suck before using two fingers to find that spot inside her that would make her scream. And she did scream. Loud. It was music to his ears and everything on him stood bigger and stronger and harder.

When her hips stopped bucking he sat up to look at her. She wasn't smiling but she looked beautiful. She used a hand to rub her face and over her hair. Blonde strands fell across her eyes and she looked so much like the old Amy of Weeping Reef. Young, carefree and in love with life Amy. And *he'd* done that. He'd made her feel that way—just for a moment.

Rising up above her, he didn't wait for her to be ready. He had to have her. *Now.* He slid in with force, grabbing her hips and forcing her back and forth. But she didn't deny him. She moved and rocked and moaned and called his name and the pressure built as she started to get control of her body. She matched him. She liked the way he moved—he could tell. She was hungry for him, greedy for him, and it just made him want her even more.

She sat up with him still inside her, her legs encircling him, her arms on his chest as his muscles moved. She watched them, watched what they were doing, and he lost it. Watching her watch made something inside his brain burst and he came without a second's hesitation.

For a moment everything went black, and Luke took the time to enjoy what had undoubtedly been the best sex of his life.

CHAPTER TEN

For Amy, the next two weeks were spent in a bubble. Working hard on her new account was easier when she knew that at the end of every day she'd get rewarded. With Luke. And his insatiable appetite…for *her*. Her body, her pleasure. He seemed to like it all.

He didn't call her during the day, but whenever she felt overwhelmed or bored, or felt like talking to him, he took her calls. He answered her texts. He paid her attention—he made her feel she was someone worth listening to and it was intoxicating. *He* was intoxicating. And the sex…

Amy shivered in her seat as she stared out through the plate glass window on the eighteenth floor of her work building. They were constantly hungry for each other. Every time was like the first time. He looked at her as if she was the most beautiful thing he'd ever seen, and she couldn't believe how much he fascinated her. She'd touched every muscle, every inch of skin on his body. She'd traced his tattoos with her finger, asking what each one meant.

She usually didn't get much of an answer, though,

because touching always turned to kissing, and kissing always turned to something more. It was wild and passionate and everything she'd never had with Laurie.

When she'd had a crush on Luke all those years ago she'd seen him as someone older, elusive and hard to pin down. Now it was different. She wasn't attracted to his cool, calm exterior any more. She was attracted to his warmth. To the way he made her feel. Alive. Buzzing.

She knew she shouldn't get too into this—he'd told her that he was only home for a little while, and reminded her plenty of times that relationships didn't work out for him because he was always travelling, but she couldn't help it. This wasn't just a fling—this was something else. They couldn't be that into each other and then let it fade away because he had to leave.

This relationship, although it was only two weeks old, felt more real than any relationship Amy had even had. She could be herself. She could expose herself and no matter what—he still wanted her. Was hungry for her. Not because he wanted to heal her or help her but just because he wanted her.

The phone in Amy's office made her head spin back to the computer and what she was working on. *Work.* She had to get back to it. She was meeting with the new clients later and they wanted to see her progress on the social media plan. Which she was nailing.

'Hey, Ames—what's up?'

Willa. Amy's heart beat a little faster. She'd been

neglecting her friend lately. Between work and Luke, she didn't have much time for their usual after-work drinks or lazy lunch dates. She needed to make it up to her.

'Heaps, darling. Working on this social media plan—it's hectic.'

'Clearly. I haven't seen you in so long I forget what you look like.'

Willa's tone was a little accusatory. Amy winced.

'I know, babe, and I'm sorry. I need to see you, but I've just been busy…you know.'

'Yeah, with work…'

'Yeah.'

'Definitely not with my brother.'

Amy stilled. That beating heart stopped. She hadn't said a word to Willa about her and Luke. She hadn't had the chance, for one—and also, if it didn't work out, she didn't want Willa to be upset. But to be honest the real reason was that this thing with Luke was new. And fragile. And so good. And she didn't want anything to touch it. She didn't want to be talked out of it. Because it was crazy, and she knew that, but she just didn't want to face it. Not yet.

'What do you mean?'

'I mean you have been spending a lot of time with Luke—haven't you?'

How the hell did she know that? Had Luke said something? Something about that idea made Amy's head and heart swell. He must like her if he was talking to his sister about them being together. What had he said?

'I… What…?'

'Jess told me.'

Jess. Of course. They'd tried to be discreet, but Jess had seen him at the flat. Leaving. Arriving. Jess had tried to ask Amy about it but she'd shut her down. She usually discussed everything with Jess—but she didn't want to discuss this with her either.

She also suspected that Jess had a bit of a crush on Luke, and although she hated to admit it she was slightly panicked by that thought. Jess was hot and fun and edgy and out there, and a part of Amy wondered if maybe Luke would prefer that, given the chance. It was a crazy thought—but Luke made her a little crazy.

'He's just popped in a few times…to talk about things. Has he been better with you?'

Turn the conversation around. That was the best solution.

'I know you're trying to turn this around to me, Ames, but we're talking about *you*. And Luke. And when he's turning up late and leaving in the morning he's not there to "talk about things", is he?'

Amy could tell Willa was a bit peeved. But she wasn't sure why. Was it because she hadn't told her what was going on or—worse—was it because she didn't approve? She'd known this would happen. Other people's opinions *always* affected things. That was why she hadn't wanted this to get out yet. She'd wanted to get to know him on her own. Enjoy him on her own. But it was out now and she'd have to deal with it.

'Don't be mad, Wills.'

'I'm not mad. Just confused. Why haven't you told me? Why does Jess know and I don't?'

That was it. Willa was worried about their friendship. Which was crazy as Willa was the best friend Amy had ever had and ever would. They'd been through so much during that summer on Weeping Reef, and since they'd become friends again it had been as if the past eight years' absence hadn't happened.

'Jess doesn't know, Wills. She's just been in the flat and seen some things and is assuming a lot. But you're right. We need to talk. But I can't today—I have a super-important meeting. How about drinks tomorrow night at Saints? I'll tell you everything then.'

Willa paused. Amy could hear her breathing. And thinking.

'Okay. But don't bail on me—or I'll hunt you down, okay?'

'Okay, I won't. See you then, my lovely.'

Amy hung up with a full heart. She had so much right now. A friend who loved and cared about her. A fabulous job. A great lifestyle. But for some reason it all paled when she thought of those times spent with Luke. He made her feel more alive and bright than anything else.

She'd never been this excited about a man and she'd never let a man's interest in her affect her other relationships or her emotions. How had Luke got under her skin so quickly? Laurie's love had been easy and secure, and she'd always known where she stood, but with Luke it was different. Every day she wondered if it was her last with him, or if it was even going anywhere.

And now people were beginning to talk. Maybe she needed to find out. As much as she wanted it to keep going on the way it was, perhaps it was time to find out if this thing they'd started was anything—or nothing. If anything, having this talk now might save her a broken heart—because she was pretty damn sure that even though she hated the idea of it she was falling like a stone in the ocean for Luke.

Luke checked his watch. She was late. He was getting used to that. She was always late. He hated it when people were late, but when it came to Amy—like everything else about her—he liked it. It added to her charm. Which was utterly stupid.

He tried to think of something he didn't like about her, but he couldn't. And that was what was annoying him. Too often lately he'd been thinking about her. He'd always made a point of not contacting the women he was sleeping with. He didn't want them to think he wanted more.

But when *she* called him or texted him he couldn't help but respond. He liked hearing her voice. He liked listening to her problems. He liked the sound of her voice. It turned him on. It calmed him down. It made him feel better. Which was why he was nervous. Letting someone else affect the way he felt was dangerous. It made him lose sight of what was going on.

He spotted her coming down the street. Her skirt

was tight and her heels were high. He loved it when she looked all professional and smart—it turned him on. But then when she was at home and in bed naked, with her hair everywhere, it turned him on as well.

Damn, *everything* about her turned him on. He needed to find something about her he didn't like. Just something small he could focus on. Because he'd realised this morning when she hadn't texted him and he'd missed it that he was feeling a little too much for little Miss Lollipop. *Big mistake.*

'How did your meeting go?'

He'd barely got the words out before she landed on him. Her arms around his neck, her soft lips on his. He liked that about her. She always wanted him. Always wanted to touch him. Always showed him how she felt. It was a nice change from most of the women he met, who preferred games over real emotion. But he was supposed to be finding things he didn't like—not things he did.

He held her arms and pushed her back. 'Did you win them over?'

She smiled. He liked that too. She had a beautiful smile. Sunny…bright. Nice straight white teeth and a dimple in either cheek.

'Of course I did. They love me. Why wouldn't they? I'm amazing.'

He liked that too. Her cheeky confidence. She never made excuses. She knew who she was and what she was and that turned him on.

This wasn't going well.

'That's true. You *are* amazing.'

She smiled and he realised he liked her eyes as well. Caramel-brown, they were looking at him softly now and his body hardened. How the hell could her damn eyes turn him on?

'But I have a surprise for you.'

She raised an eyebrow. Yep. Turned on.

'I like surprises…'

She held his hand and rose up on her toes to kiss his cheek. This was a disaster. But he was about to give her a surprise he was sure she *wouldn't* like. Then he might see another side of her. Bitchy. Moody. Inflexible.

He pulled her to the side of the road. 'I'm taking you for a ride.'

She turned to where he was looking. His fully customised 1975 Harley Fat Boy sat arrogantly on the road. A motorbike. This would test her. Riding a bike with him would mess up her hair. She was wearing heels. Her skirt was too tight. She would complain. Most women did.

Amy let go of his hand. She stepped off the kerb, her eyes trailing over the length of the bike. She reached out a hand tentatively and stroked the custom-painted tank. Luke had built the bike himself. He'd taken pains to remove everything nice on the original bike. Everything on it now was raw, pared back, and as un-pretty as he'd been able to make it. This wasn't a show bike. It roared. It cut through the traffic like a beast. It was a hog and a pig and he loved it. But he was sure she wouldn't.

'Wow.'

His heart sank. Was that a sarcastic 'wow'? He had wanted to pick her up on the bike today so he'd see that bad side of her, but now that she'd said it he realised he was a little disappointed.

'You don't like it?'

She turned to him. 'It's magnificent. It's so...*you*. Are you going to let me ride on it with you?'

Luke's heart stopped. She *liked* it. She wanted to ride it with him.

He should have known. That reckless, carefree Amy was still in there. All locked up behind her power suits and bravado—but she was still there. Still looking for new adventures.

His blood bubbled. She wanted to ride and he wanted to show her. He wanted her to feel the way he did on a bike. When his mind clicked off and the wind and the speed made his heart race and he felt fearless and immortal. She'd love that.

But this was supposed to frighten her. She was supposed to complain. This was supposed to be the thing he didn't like about her. She'd surprised him once again. And it turned him on.

If it wasn't for all the people walking along the street right now he'd rip that tight skirt right off her, lay her on his bike and show her how much he liked her right here.

The beast she'd awakened in him growled and he beat it down with a whip. His attraction to her was getting dangerous and it had already been two weeks. It was time for him to move on, get distracted, feel suffocated. But he hadn't yet. And that was irritating him. Maybe it was just because he wasn't working all day long. Usually he had that to focus on.

'The helmet will mess your hair up—just warning you.'

She stepped closer, her hands on his chest, and looked up at him. 'I'm not scared of getting my hair messed up.'

'What *are* you scared of, then?'

Her eyes flicked from one of his to another. She was thinking about her answer.

'I'm scared of lots of things, but not when I'm with you.'

Her answer was quiet and her voice had changed. He felt it, stabbing right in his heart. Another thing he liked. She liked him. But that was exactly the thing he *shouldn't* like.

'We'll see about that. I've heard it's pretty scary on the back of my bike.'

She smiled and reached around to the back of her skirt. There was a long zipper there that she zipped right up. She took the helmet from his hands and put it over her head. She fumbled with the clasp, so Luke reached out and did it up for her. He didn't want her to hurt herself if she fell off. Which she wouldn't. He was an excellent rider.

He took her handbag and stuffed it in his saddlebag. He really pushed it down but she didn't complain. She just raised an eyebrow as he hauled himself on to the bike. She didn't even ask any questions. She just slipped off her shoes, shoved them into the bag as well and climbed on the back.

Luke pumped the peg. Her breasts were firm against his back. He pumped again and the engine roared into life. He let the clutch go and the bike jerked, throwing her forward a little until she was pressed right up against him. He couldn't see, but he was sure that skirt of hers was high up around her thighs. She tightened her grip on him with her legs and slipped her arms around his waist. His fists tightened on the grips.

He needed to ride. He had to stop thinking about her and the way she felt against his back. So trusting and so close. He just wanted to ride back to his place and get her naked—but he wasn't going to. He'd just find more things to like about her. The way she looked with nothing on, the way her skin felt—silky and smooth—and the noises she made. The soft moans and the loud screams. He liked it all.

He needed to lose himself in the wind and the speed and pretend that everything was all right and he had everything under control. So he rode. And she pressed herself closer, hugging him harder on the corners and yelling in his ear at the traffic lights. And he liked her even more. She was having fun, and she got it.

When they hit the open road her grip relaxed and she stayed quiet, and he enjoyed the feel of her pressed up hard against him as if they were one body, riding free. No destination in mind, just enjoying the ride.

Amy felt more free on the back of Luke's bike than she had in longer than she could remember. With the rush of wind flying past her ears there was no chance to talk. And there was no reason to either. They didn't need to talk. She sat close to him on the bike, every part of her pressed against him and buzzing with the road underneath. It felt intimate and comfortable.

Every bump or turn in the road just brought her closer to him and she snuggled in tight. But not too tight. Her grip was firm, but he was able to move and guide her if he needed to. They were in unison, in perfect sync, and Amy realised that this was what she'd never had with Laurie.

She had never been Laurie's equal. He'd loved her too much and had put her on a pedestal so high that she'd never have been able to love him that much. But here with Luke she felt as if they both knew what was going on and they both wanted the same thing. Today. With each other. On this bike. In the sun.

She wasn't sure how long they'd been riding. The sun was still up, but falling, and Luke had slowed down to manoeuvre through the gates of the national park. There was a track, but the trees were close. It twisted and turned but strangely Amy felt safe. She never felt as if she'd hit one of those trees. He knew what he was doing and she completely trusted him as a rider.

The bike stopped and Amy still buzzed. She climbed off a little shakily, and Luke caught her and laughed.

'Might take you a few minutes to get your land legs. Sit down and take your helmet off. I want to show you something.'

Amy sat, a smile planted firmly on her face. She had no idea where she was but she didn't care. Adventure. Fun. Mystery. Excitement. That was what was missing from her life. She'd been playing it safe for so long she'd forgotten what this was like. This was the sort of thing she'd done all the time on Weeping Reef—she'd always been looking for something to make her heart beat faster.

She guessed her need for excitement was due to the safe and fairly subdued way she'd grown up, in a house full of loving and gentle health nuts and the safe but so confining all-girls school she'd gone to. It was no wonder she'd broken out and gone crazy on Weeping Reef. It had been the first time she'd met people who were like her. People who wanted to have fun and see the world and have adventures.

And they'd all had some fun. Until that night. When everything had changed. When fun had seemed to die.

Amy watched Luke as he rested his helmet on the seat and pulled a knapsack out of the leather bag tied to the side of the bike. Luke was one of only two people who knew what had happened that night. Amy had never told her parents or Laurie. Her mother had suspected that something had happened on the island, and one night she'd come close to guessing, but she hadn't, and Amy had been relieved.

She didn't want to reveal how naïve and stupid she'd been and she didn't want to talk about it. All she wanted to do was forget. She knew now it wasn't her fault. But somewhere deep inside she had one regret.

That she'd left. That she'd packed up and run away and hadn't confronted the man who'd affected her so much. That she hadn't told him what she thought of him and what a coward he was. Somehow, in some way, it made her feel that he'd won and she'd lost.

'Ready?'

Luke smiled and Amy's mood brightened instantly. He grabbed her hand and hauled her up easily from the rock she was sitting on. The day was warm, but not hot, and they were alone in the bushland. Sticks and dry leaves crunched underfoot and the only other sound was the calling of birds and cicadas as they pushed their way through the low-lying branches.

A hum was the first indication that the landscape was changing, and it was only seconds later that Amy had to stop and look.

'Luke, it's beautiful…' she said absently.

Falling from a cut of rock high above them was a large waterfall. It wasn't blue, but nor was it green, and it didn't rush down heavily but fell gently, with occasional rushing swoops into a pool below that was surrounded by rocks. The water created an atmosphere of cool air that Amy felt whisper over her shoulders.

'My dad used to bring me here when I was young. We'd ride all day and camp here at night. Back then you could light fires, so we'd cook up some sausages and talk about nothing.'

'Do you two come here any more?'

'No. We haven't been back since Mum died.'

Amy remembered Willa talking about her mother a

few times. She'd died when Willa was in high school. It had been hard for her. Luke had been away at university and she'd been alone with her dad, who had been grieving.

She'd told Amy how alone she'd felt. Amy had always imagined that they had become so close because Willa had been dying for some female company. When they'd first met Willa had been so shy and reserved. It had been fun to try and bring her out of her shell and make her see the world differently.

Amy was sure she'd done most of her outrageous things just to show off to Willa. And of course to Luke. Perhaps that was why Luke hadn't liked her back then. Perhaps he'd thought his sister should have been cocooned for longer instead of being thrown out into the big bad world and encouraged to live the way Amy wanted to.

Back then Amy had been looking for fun without thinking of the consequences. Now all she did was think of consequences. She wondered if there was some way to find a balance. A way to have fun, like she was having with Luke, but still be good at her job and feel safe. She felt safe right now. Holding his hand, enjoying the sun. She felt safer with him—a man she'd really only known properly for two weeks—than she had with any man she'd met since Laurie.

And the difference was that she wanted Luke so badly she ached. He seemed like the perfect combination of sexual freedom and safety. Except he wasn't. Because he'd told her so many times that he didn't do relationships, and she still wasn't sure that going out with her best friend's brother was her smartest idea, so how was *that* safe? But right now she didn't want to think about that. She just wanted to enjoy what was left of the afternoon with Luke.

Amy's body shimmered in the water. It hadn't taken much convincing for her to get naked and dive in. She was brave and bold and game for anything. She surprised Luke every time. She was thirsty for adventure, but never reckless about it. And sexually she wanted to do whatever it took to please him—just as he wanted to do whatever it took to please her.

He was sure he just had—on the riverbank. Now it was her turn. She turned back to him, a sexy half-smile on her face as she cut through the water with long, confident strokes, only coming up for air when she was near the waterfall. She dipped her hands in it, then gasped when she tried to put her head under and it pushed her down into the water.

He was at her side in seconds, pulling her up from where she'd sunk. She coughed and spluttered and pushed the hair out of her eyes. He pulled her close. He wanted her where he could see her. Where he could keep her safe.

Her breasts pushed up against his chest and her legs wrapped around him. She totally trusted him. She didn't for a second think he'd break her heart, and that made him feel a little too hot. She smiled slowly and he kissed her, long and hard. He let his tongue stroke against hers and moved against the smooth skin of her legs.

This afternoon had been perfect, and he didn't want it to end, but it had to. And so did this thing with Amy. Not because he'd found anything wrong with her, but because he *couldn't* find anything wrong with her. There was only ever one reason a man couldn't find fault with a girl, and that was… Well, it was better not to think about that.

Suddenly Amy's eyes went dark and the smile disappeared from her face as she shifted to allow his length inside her. He knew he was so close it was dangerous. Amy moaned as he moved to fill her and her fingernails scraped over his back. The pain from the scratches felt good, and pressure built from feeling her move against him.

He needed traction, so he moved them back towards the rocks underneath the waterfall. Grabbing her by the waist, he lifted her up and off him and onto the rocks. She lay back, waiting like a beautiful mermaid. He wanted her. Had to have her. He wanted her body and to hear her laugh and to keep her safe. And as he climbed up on top of her, to slide in long and smooth and slow, he knew he was falling.

This couldn't go on.

She groaned in appreciation.

This had to end.

She lifted herself up and wrapped her arms around his neck. He pushed himself in deeper. Her moans got louder, her panting wilder. and he couldn't stop. He watched her face, her eyes—the way she threw her head back to expose the bones at the base of her neck and her hard nipples. He kissed them. He kissed her neck and behind her ear. He found her mouth and kissed away her screams as he allowed himself to go, allowed himself to love her—just once.

And when he came to and saw her breathing heavily, her skin glistening, not smiling, exhausted from their lovemaking, he knew it had to end.

CHAPTER ELEVEN

THE MESSAGE ON Luke's phone beeped angrily at him.

Huynh has revoked the approval. Everything has to be submitted again.

Kel Huynh had been the thorn in his ass since this whole project began. She was tough and strict and had made him jump through every hoop she could find during the whole process of building his hotel.

It was his most ambitious project to date. He'd never built a hotel this large or complicated before. There was a retail precinct, bars, restaurants, and he'd managed to lease out a large portion of the hotel to one of the richest companies in South East Asia to open their state-of-the-art casino. But Kel Huynh had fought him every inch of the way.

She was against the casino, but without it the project wasn't feasible. They'd managed to get the casino in, but now she was stopping them getting a twenty-four-hour licence—which would totally ruin the whole project.

His man in Singapore was one of his most trusted employees. He'd managed and transformed Luke's very first hotel and Luke knew he'd be able to handle this on his own. But it irritated him that there was another hitch. Maybe it could be sorted without him... but maybe a trip back to Singapore was just what he needed. Distance. Time. Perspective.

This afternoon at the waterfall with Amy had been awesome. For the first time in a long time he'd thought of nothing else but now. But that didn't sound too smart to him.

He'd always been a planner. He'd always planned for the future, tried to foresee problems before they happened so he could deal with them. So he could be prepared. So much in life was unpredictable—planning was his way of trying to stay in control. But with Amy he didn't even think about planning. Each day was a new adventure. And despite what he knew he should do it felt great to be living in the moment. Too great. Dangerously great.

'What is it?'

Amy was pulling on her helmet. She'd forgone the skirt this time and was planning to ride behind him in nothing but her underwear and his shirt tied around her waist. With her wet hair drying messily and her shirt unbuttoned to reveal a slice of her gorgeous breasts, she looked hotter than he'd ever seen her.

'There's a problem with the Singapore hotel. A big one.'

'What's wrong?'

'It's the twenty-four-hour opening. They've denied our licence. It's a big problem.'

'But haven't you got someone to handle all that for you?'

'It's a big problem, Amy—the whole project could fall.'

A slight exaggeration, but he needed to buy some time. She put her hands on her hips and let her head fall to the side. Hot. Sexy. He wanted her again.

'I might have to go back to Singapore.'

'What?' She stood up straighter. 'When?'

'Soon. Tomorrow.'

He knew they could handle it without him. But he also knew no one else could do it better than him. Kel Huynh was clever and she was quick. He really should be there in the room when his people met with her.

'I've never been to Singapore.'

Luke stilled. Amy's expression had changed. She stood awkwardly, her hands clasped in front of her.

'I've always wanted to.'

'It's… I wouldn't say it's the most exciting city.'

Bars, restaurants, a nightlife like no other, constant warm weather—the place was exactly up Amy's alley.

But if she was there he wouldn't be able to think. Or work. This crazy feeling of falling for her would never go away and he needed it to. This was *Amy*. Little Amy. His sister's best friend. Reckless, careless Amy, who would get hurt when he let her down. He couldn't fall for Amy.

'I don't know—I've heard good things. And it would be really helpful to see a hotel of your size in action. To help with my account, I mean…' Her caramel eyes looked at him, then looked at the ground. 'Unless, I mean… Unless you don't want me tagging along. I shouldn't—'

'No, it's not that. I… It's just. I'll be working and I won't have a lot of time to…spend with you.'

'No. Of course…I know.' She looked up again. 'But I'm a big girl—I could look after myself.'

The silence went on too long.

Luke didn't know what to say without sounding like the world's biggest ass

'Okay, yeah. Sure. You can come…if you want.'

She shrugged and her cheeks reddened. 'Only if you want me to.'

'Of course…'

Luke moved to put his arm around her waist. He went to kiss her forehead but she thought he was going to kiss her lips and moved, but not fast enough, and he ended up kissing her eyelid instead. *Smooth*.

'Of course I want you to.'

'Okay…then…'

The ride back to Amy's apartment was quiet. She didn't yell in his ear at the traffic lights and she didn't press herself up against him. When she got off she thanked him and retrieved her bag and skirt with an awkward blush.

Luke's palms itched. He didn't want it to be like this. Even though he knew they couldn't go on, he didn't want it to be like *this*. But it was. And it was probably going to be like this for a week, because now she was coming to Singapore with him.

'I'll have someone book a flight for you and let you know the details.'

He kissed her on the cheek. She didn't look at him.

'Okay, sure. No problem. I'll wait to hear from you then.'

'Good.'

'Great.'

'Okay, then. Bye.'

'Bye.'

When Luke's motorcycle had roared into life and sped down the street Amy lifted her expensive handbag above her head and threw it onto the ground with a force she hadn't realised she had. Then she swore so badly she was sure it would have made a trucker blush. Then she picked up her bag and her pride and stalked into her house to find as much wine as she could and shout at herself for being such a fool.

The sweat dripped slowly between Amy's shoulder-blades and down her back. The taxi was clean, but there was no air con. She was hot and tired and re-gretting everything.

She knew she looked a wreck. Frizzy hair, make-up sweated off and massive bags under her eyes.

The eight-hour flight from Sydney to Singapore had been awkward and embarrassing. First class was always a nice way to travel, but Amy hadn't been able to enjoy it. Luke had spent the entire trip next to her on his computer, sending emails and filling out forms.

Amy had tried to talk to him but he'd shut her

down with one-word answers and she'd spent the entire trip feeling as if she was disturbing him.

Everything had been going so well. They'd been enjoying each other. She'd been happy and he'd seemed happy. It hadn't been until she'd asked to come to Singapore with him that everything had changed. But why shouldn't she have come? They'd spent almost every day together in the past two weeks, and he'd seemed to be as into her as she was him.

But obviously she'd got it wrong. *Again*. She'd trusted someone she shouldn't have *again*.

The taxi stopped in front of a tall space-age style building. Luke was still silent as he stepped out of the taxi and ordered the bags to be brought in. As soon as the doors rolled open he was met by five staff members and Amy found herself walking behind him. Forgotten. Neglected. This wasn't the Luke of the last two weeks. Who *was* this man? This seemed more like Weeping Reef Luke. Absent and obsessed with work.

Check-in took no time. Luke was handed a key, and he finally took Amy's arm as he led her to the elevator.

'What do you think?' he asked when they stepped into the cool mirrored lift.

She shook her hair out, confused. 'About...?'

'The hotel. Do you like it?'

Did she like the hotel? *That* was what he wanted to talk about after an eight-hour silent flight?

'Sure. It's amazing.'

It was. From the garden in the foyer to the busy,

efficient service of the staff. But she hadn't expected anything less of any hotel Luke owned.

'Good.'

More silence. The lift stopped on the very top floor. Of course. The doors opened to reveal a private penthouse. Of course. Amy should have felt better about it than she did. They were here in one of the most exciting cities in the world in possibly the most beautiful hotel room she'd ever seen and she wasn't happy. She was furious.

'I have some work to do. I'll have to go into the office. There's food and drinks in the fridge—help yourself and call the concierge if you need anything at all.'

That was it. That was the very limit.

'What I *need*, Luke, is for you to stop acting like the King of Jerks and talk to me.'

He looked at her blankly and her anger spread.

'Or is this how it's going to be? You avoiding me and neglecting me and treating me like some mistress? Because that's not good enough, Luke. I'm not your mistress. I'm not here for a sordid little affair. I want to be with you and spend time with you and that's exactly what's going to happen!'

Amy didn't expect what happened next. She didn't expect him to come at her with force and grab her around the waist and kiss her with a passion she hadn't felt before—even from him.

'Luke?' She tried to speak between kisses.

'I thought you were regretting your decision to

come here,' he said, coming up for air before putting her face in his hands and kissing her again.

'I thought *you* were.'

'No. Not at all. I *want* you here. I want you with me. I couldn't stand you not talking to me on the plane.'

Amy clawed at his shirt. She needed him naked. His desperation for her was turning her on.

'You were the one not talking to me.'

'No, that was *you*.'

He tugged at her top until it came off over her head and she desperately unbuttoned his shirt. He pulled it free and she moved to his belt as he pulled her pants off easily. She stepped out of them and gasped when his hand drifted down her stomach and into her underwear, his fingers gently coaxing her to come to life. It didn't take much. She was already hot and wet for him as she fumbled with the remainder of his clothes.

'Why are you so difficult?' she demanded as his fingers expertly drove inside her.

She clung to his shoulders, then let her teeth clamp on his lips as they kissed. His moan echoed in her ear and spun her brain out of control. His skin was hot and he was naked now. She could feel him hard and ready against her belly. She couldn't wait for a bed. She wanted him now. Eight hours on the plane—not touching him, not talking to him, not having him close to her—and she was mad with anger and desire and want. Apparently he felt the same way.

'Not difficult. Maybe a little challenging. But you

seem like the type of woman who likes a challenge,' he answered, lifting her up with one arm and pulling her underwear down with the other.

She hoisted her legs around his waist before sliding her hand down his taut torso and letting her fingers grip his silky shaft. She knew what it felt like, what it tasted like, and she wanted it inside her right now.

'There's challenging, and then there's downright rude. You didn't talk to me for *eight hours*, Luke. You made me feel rejected and unwanted.'

She squeezed and his arms held her tighter, his eyes meeting hers. Hot. Direct.

'I'm sorry. Sometimes when I don't know what to say I say nothing.' He kissed her shoulders, then lifted her up a little to kiss her breasts.

Amy used both her hands to cup his face—she needed him to hear what she had to say. 'You can say anything to me, Luke. *Anything*. Even if you think I don't want to hear it. The worst thing you can do is leave me in the dark. Then I jump to conclusions and I get scared—and I hate being scared.'

He stilled and she felt his big arms pull her in closer. His forehead was close to hers…their lips were almost touching.

'Don't be scared, Amy. I have you.'

Amy couldn't hold back any more. The tight knot in her heart was taking up all the space and her heart was beating hard and heavy. She kissed him desperately, wanting him to know exactly how she felt right then.

'I know you do,' she murmured as his kisses became deeper and even more frantic.

'Say you want me, Amy.' His demand was growled in her ear.

'No, you say it first.' She was throbbing for him. She wanted his length where his fingers had moved and were now eagerly exploring.

He leaned down, let his tongue slide on her earlobe and growled in a deep, gritty voice, 'I want you.'

Every thought left Amy's head.

'Now,' she demanded. 'Now!'

Luke lifted her at the waist and let her slide onto him. He was big and hard and he filled her, and she wanted more. She moved up and down and around until the heat inside her body coiled in her core. This was what she'd missed. Him being close. Him needing her and wanting her and depending on her.

She massaged his big shoulders and whispered in his ear, using the dirtiest words she knew. That seemed to fuel him even more and he drove himself into her almost angrily, definitely greedily, and Amy took his anger and his greed and paid it back just as violently.

Luke brought out something in her she'd never felt before—a desire to please and be pleased. A need to protect and take care of someone. As selfishly as she enjoyed sex with him, the desire to give herself selflessly to him was almost impossible to control. She was doing things with Luke she'd never done with Laurie. She'd never whispered dirty words to him.

She'd never wanted Laurie so much she couldn't wait even to lie down.

Luke was different. He made her feel as if nothing was taboo. As if sex was a normal—no, a vital part of their relationship and was the way they communicated sometimes. Sex was like breathing and eating and talking. It kept them close and together and sane and made her feel that they needed each other the way they needed food.

Luke was moving slowly now and she knew what was happening. It was his calm before the storm. His way of preparing himself before using all his strength. And she knew this was her time to let go and feel him rubbing so close, making her clit come alive, making her orgasm bubble to the surface. She rode him and he rode her right back.

'I'm coming,' he growled, and she responded with more dirty words. More reasons for him to use all the strength he had to take her to the place only he could.

This time the orgasm lasted longer, and the aftershocks kept her clinging to him for minutes. She couldn't let go. Their bodies were almost fused together. It took a while for their breathing to calm and for a laugh to escape from both of them.

'*That* was an orgasm,' he said, his voice deep and sleepy.

Slowly, carefully, he let her off and she found the chaise longue that sat nearby and collapsed onto it. He collapsed next to her and kissed her mouth before shifting to one side and running the backs of his knuckles up and down her arm.

'Don't ever do that again,' she said, still breathless and panting.

'What?'

'Leave it that long before making love to me. I'm pretty sure I lost some brain cells then.'

He laughed, and the sound warmed her from the inside out. She loved it that she could make him laugh.

'Me too. It was pretty intense.'

'It was—because you ignored me for so long.'

'No, you ignored *me*. I was trying everything I could to feel your leg under that blanket.'

Amy furrowed her brow. 'That's what you were doing? I thought you were pushing my leg away.'

'No, you ratbag.' He turned to face her and his arms came around her as her body sank into comfortable relief. 'I was trying it on. Trust me, if you feel my hands anywhere near you I'm trying it on. Never pushing you away.'

'Then you should *say* that and not let me jump to conclusions.'

'You should ask and not let me think you don't want to talk.'

Touché.

They lay like that for a long time, drifting in and out of sleep. Exhausted from lovemaking and being wound up and from the flight.

After a while, they got hungry, and Luke insisted on ordering food from Din Tai Fung. He wanted her to have the dumplings, insisting they were the best. And they were. And they ate and talked and laughed and watched as the sun set over Singapore's skyline.

As they sat together, their legs entwined, full of dumplings and content from hot sex, Amy's shoulders relaxed. Luke was asking her about why she'd left Melbourne and what she'd left behind.

'His name was Laurie...' she explained. She hadn't talked about him to Luke yet. She hadn't wanted him to know. She was worried he'd judge her as everyone else had. 'His parents were good friends with my parents, which was why my leaving became so messy.'

'Messy how?'

Amy remembered the sadness and the anger and the guilt she'd felt. It hadn't happened overnight with Laurie—it had taken a while. It had started with little things. Things that had annoyed her about him. Mostly the way he had become so dependent on her. She'd started to feel suffocated and as if she couldn't make a move without it affecting him. She'd thought that sex with Laurie had been great at the time. It wasn't until now, when she'd had sex with Luke, that she realised how safe and staid it had been.

Amy snuggled in closer. 'Our break-up wasn't just about the two of us. Our families got involved...everyone had an opinion. It was actually my brother who helped me make my mind up. He said that if I wanted to leave he would be there for me. That he was on my side and it was better for everyone if I listened to myself and what I wanted. He said they'd get over it eventually.'

'And have they?'

'My mother was angry about it for a long time, but she loves me. I know that, and I know she wants me to be happy. So she doesn't even talk about it now—except to occasionally mention that she runs into Laurie from time to time.'

'And how did he take it? Laurie?'

'Badly. He begged me to come back. Cried. Wrote me letters. Posted sad quotes on social media. I almost caved so many times, but Antony told me to stay strong. He said that life is yours to live—not anybody else's. He said I wouldn't ever be happy if I didn't do what my heart wanted and that eventually my unhappiness would start to affect everyone else. He told me that it was just the change—the prospect of everything being turned upside down—that was making everyone so upset, not the fact that I wanted to leave.'

'And did it make you happy? Leaving?' Luke asked quietly.

Amy felt his hands start to stroke her hair and she felt almost like a cat, curled up and comfortable and not wanting to move an inch.

Yes. She was happy right now. She'd been so happy since she'd met Luke again. For the first time in a long time she didn't feel the need to go anywhere, see anyone or do anything. She didn't need anything to make her feel high, to make her forget. She just wanted to be here with him. Still.

'I will be,' she said quietly. 'What about you? I don't know anything about your significant relationships.'

Luke breathed in heavily and stopped stroking her head. She didn't move an inch. She wanted him to keep going. After a few seconds he did and she breathed out, curling up even closer to him.

'There was one of significance. Well, our *relationship* wasn't significant. We didn't know each other long. I was in Malaysia for business and we met at a business dinner. She was English—divorced. She'd been living in Malaysia for six years. She needed company. I needed…well…I needed company too. It lasted three weeks. I liked her a lot but there was no real connection there. We were just friends.'

'Why was it significant, then?'

'She got pregnant.'

Amy froze. *Luke had a child?* How had she not known this?

'She lost the baby, though. At fourteen weeks. I wasn't there when it happened.'

Amy sat up and looked at him. His eyes were red and he looked tired. He ran a hand through his hair, messing it up. It made him look younger. Unsure of himself.

'It was a pretty bad time,' was all he said.

Amy didn't know what to say but she knew what to do. She kissed him. Lightly, gently. And he kissed her back. 'I'm sorry, Luke.'

Luke's smile was small, but it was there. He pulled her back to where she'd been lying and started stroking her hair again.

'It happens all the time, apparently,' he murmured, in a tone that plainly said even if it did, it still wasn't fair.

'Do you still talk to her?'

'Koko? No. Not any more. It happened over a year ago. She's married again now—or so I heard.'

Amy suspected he hadn't 'heard' at all. She suspected he kept a close eye on Koko. Because that was what Luke did.

'It's hard to lose someone. Especially a child.'

'No one should have to lose a child,' Luke said quietly, his hands steady in her hair.

'It must have brought back memories for you.'

His hand stopped. 'Memories?'

'About your mother…'

His silence made her fear she'd said the wrong thing.

She stayed still. 'I'm sorry, Luke, I didn't mean to…'

'No, no, it's okay. I just…I haven't talked about… Mum…in a long time.'

'You don't have to if you don't want to.'

'No.' He began stroking her again but adjusted his legs and she moved, giving him more room. 'It's okay. It was a long time ago. I was an adult when it happened. Willa felt it more than me.'

'Nineteen must have been a hard age to lose your mother. Isn't that when you were away at college?'

'Yeah, I was at university and getting involved in hotel management. I'd been working in hotels throughout school. Mum got sick while I was away. I wasn't there when…when it happened. Afterwards, Dad suggested I stay away. He said it would take my mind off things.'

'That's an odd thing for him to suggest, don't you

think? Wouldn't it have been better if you'd stayed with your family?'

'I should have been there for them before. I suppose Dad thought I may as well make something of myself, seeing as I'd already missed my last opportunity to see Mum. It didn't really affect me the way it did Willa. I didn't miss her like she did.'

Amy turned again to look at him and he looked down at her. The sadness in his eyes didn't match his words. He'd missed her. And by the look on his face he still did.

'You didn't do anything wrong, Luke. You were young and you were living the life you needed to live. Your mother would have been proud of you.'

'You don't know that.' His words were abrupt. He shifted.

'You don't still feel guilty about anything that happened do you?'

This time he shifted again—hard. He lifted his arm and checked his watch. 'This has been nice, Amy…too nice. I really do have to work while I'm here.'

The change of subject took her by surprise. Amy moved so he could free his legs. 'Now?'

'Now. Sorry. I really do.'

He stopped to kiss her. Long and hard and sincere. It soothed her a little. But only a little. She wrapped her arms around herself as he jumped off the chaise longue and padded into the shower. It didn't take him long and he emerged fresh and clean as if it were the morning. But it wasn't—it was almost six o'clock in the evening.

'There's a rooftop bar in the hotel. Get dressed and go up there. I should only be a couple of hours and I'll meet you, okay?'

He pushed his tie up to his throat and kissed her cheek and in seconds he was gone. Just like that. As if the past few hours hadn't happened.

He left Amy feeling a little cold and very confused.

The lights that had seemed so pretty—almost magical a few hours ago—were now burning holes in her retinas. He still wasn't back.

Amy flung back the remains of the fruity cocktail she was drinking. She'd lost count at four. He was silent and absent and neglecting her again. He hadn't been like this in Sydney. In Sydney he'd been attentive and sweet and…*present*. They'd been in Singapore no more than a few hours and already he was gone—neglecting her again as he had on the plane. She'd made it clear that she hated silence. He knew she'd start to get scared if he didn't let her know what was going on in his head.

Amy checked her phone again. No messages. No Snapchats. Nothing. He'd said he would meet her in a couple of hours. It was now almost ten o'clock.

Amy held her hand up to gain the attention of the waiter. She needed another drink. She shifted and smoothed down the cool jersey fabric of her dress. He had no idea how good she looked right now. Because if he did he'd be here—buying her drinks and paying her attention. Not neglecting her. Making her feel as he had on the plane—as if she was invisible and unimportant.

The waiter appeared with another cocktail and she stared into it. What was she doing here? Getting angry...jumping to conclusions.

This had started as an innocent fling with someone from her past. She hadn't wanted to hope that it could go anywhere, but now... After spending so much time with him, and after their conversation earlier, she knew that hope had burrowed itself deep into her heart. She wanted him and she wanted this, and if she didn't sort out what was going on she knew she'd end up with a broken heart. And after the whole disastrous Laurie business she wasn't sure she could handle that.

She knew Luke had changed. The cold, distant boy had grown into a warm and passionate man. But there was still some of the lonely workaholic buried there. Someone who was used to being on his own and who got uncomfortable if he felt someone was getting too close. That was why he'd fled earlier.

Or maybe he was avoiding her because he didn't want this to turn into anything. He hadn't wanted her to come over here in the first place. Perhaps he wasn't scared of relationships but of a relationship with *her*. He knew who she was. Who she'd been. He knew her deepest, darkest secrets. Perhaps he couldn't take this or her seriously because deep down he still believed her to be the silly party girl she'd been eight years ago.

Amy swallowed to moisten her dry throat. Her past had finally caught up with her. She'd spent the last eight years running and hiding but now it had caught up. She was all exposed, out in the open, and she felt eighteen again. Young. Naïve. Scared and not knowing what to do next.

Amy stood and grabbed at her shawl and clutch. She wasn't eighteen again. She *wasn't*. She was twenty-six. Things had changed—she'd changed. She'd grown up, even though she didn't feel she had sometimes. She knew what she wanted. She wanted Luke and she didn't want to do anything stupid again. Like trying to make him jealous.

If her past had taught her anything it was that she should tell people how she felt and not try and manipulate them with jealousy and mixed messages and silence. Bad things happened when you did that. It was time to be direct with Luke. If he was avoiding her because he didn't want to be with her she needed to know. Before she got in any deeper. Before she started to think crazy things like he actually felt something for her.

She escaped the darkness of the bar and travelled down quickly in the elevator. Her heels clacked across the paved footpath.

She checked her phone. GPS said his office was just four blocks away. Four blocks for her to figure out what she was going to say. Four blocks until she told him that she needed to know what was going on. Four blocks and she was going to tell him how she felt. And he needed to tell her too.

There was a time to be working but this wasn't it. She knew he was using his work as a sort of emotional shield. This was classic old Luke. For all his appearance of changing and maturing, becoming a man who'd dealt with his past, he was still haunted by it. Was working too hard to avoid dealing with things. Like he had at Weeping Reef.

Luke had all but admitted earlier that he'd felt shut out when his mother died. His father had spent all his time worrying about Willa, which had left no one to worry about Luke. A man who'd hidden his emotions and feelings about his mother's death by burying himself in studying and then working himself into the ground ever since.

That was why he hadn't participated in the staff's lives back on Weeping Reef. That was why he'd partied with them all but had always left when they'd got drunk and started talking about their feelings. That was why he'd done nothing when he'd seen her and Justin together that night. Denial. Emotional avoidance.

She should have seen it long ago. Her marketing training had given her the ability to peg everyone's consumer behaviour. She should have seen that Luke wasn't buying into love or even close emotional relationships because he couldn't deal with them. Willa, his father, his staff and his friends…and now her.

It wasn't fair. He'd made her feel as if he actually *felt* something for her, but he wasn't going to take it anywhere. She could see that now. He would just keep pushing her away because he didn't want to get close to her. She'd revealed herself to him over the last two weeks. He'd known her emotionally, mentally and physically in more ways than any other man ever had—even Laurie.

And now he was pushing her away. As if all of that didn't matter. As if she couldn't be trusted with his feelings. She'd trusted him with her deepest, darkest secret and he didn't trust her. How. Dared. He?

CHAPTER TWELVE

THERE WAS NO WAY Amy could have told anyone how she'd covered those few blocks to Luke's office. She wasn't sure how she'd made it there herself. But she was mad. Mad at Luke for putting her off and not having enough respect to let her in on what he was thinking. Mad at her family and Laurie for making her feel so bad about wanting more—about wanting to leave them to make the life that *she* wanted, not the one they wanted. And mad at the man who had attacked her.

He was the one who made doubts creep into her mind when they shouldn't. He was the loser who'd taken her to the beach that night when she was full of booze and tried to have sex with her when she wasn't ready.

He'd called her a tease. A slut. He'd told her she deserved it when he'd pushed her down onto the sand and pulled his jeans down. He'd hissed angrily in her ear as he'd pushed her head closer to his penis. And she'd been too young to be angry. All she'd been was terrified.

She'd pushed and shoved and kicked and screamed and yelled until finally she'd got away. And after that she'd felt nothing but guilt and shame. As if she'd done something wrong. But she hadn't. Walking to the beach with him that night and kissing him had never been an invitation. They were human beings, not animals, and when she'd said no he should have respected it.

But he hadn't. He hadn't respected what she'd wanted. Neither had Laurie and now neither did Luke.

Amy was shaking by the time she found Luke's building and pushed open the door. It was late, but there were still people around. She found the name of his company on the list and pushed the 'up' button for the lift.

Luke was *not* going to disrespect her. He was going to listen whether he liked it or not. He was going to hear what she wanted and he was going to give it to her—or at least give her a reason why he couldn't.

The lift was empty when she stepped in and pushed the button.

He had work to do—she understood that. Her own career was hectic, and she knew how easy it was to neglect your relationships when you needed to work. But that shouldn't happen. Everyone needed a life outside of work. Otherwise work was pointless. Life was no fun without friends and family and people to share it with.

Maybe Luke didn't realise that yet. Tonight he was going to learn that lesson.

The foyer of Luke's office was deserted. The lights

in the area behind the reception desk were off. Amy headed towards the light down the hall, her heels muffled on the carpet.

She heard his voice before she saw him.

'We've been over this a dozen times. Our staff numbers have *not* escalated. The figure we gave you at the start of the year is the same. We've hired additional contractors for the build, that's all.'

A pause.

'As I discussed with your planning manager, we've got that organised. We're just waiting on supplies.'

Another pause.

'Ms Huynh, I respect your policies, but this has gone on for three months. I'm losing money and this project is in danger of falling over. I understand that… I respect that, but… Yes. I understand. I will take care of it and have it to you within the hour. Goodbye.'

When Luke looked up he jumped in his chair.

'Amy! What are you doing here? I didn't hear you.'

Luke's hair was askew, as if he'd run his hands through it a million times. His eyes were lined with red streaks and his tie was off. He looked tired. Overwhelmed. The words that Amy had been practising evaporated. Luke was stressed—she could see that. She knew how that felt. When there were a dozen things to achieve and you felt as if you were the only one who could do them. As if the weight of the world was on your shoulders. She understood his need to get his work done.

It wasn't fair of him to exclude her, but when she

saw him smile she knew she wasn't ready to give up on him. Without speaking Amy walked to his side and turned his chair to face her.

'What are you doing here? I'm sorry this is taking so long, Amy. You look gorgeous... What time is it?' He glanced at his watch. 'Damn. I'm sorry, babe.' He put his hands on her hips and met her eyes. 'I'm *sorry.*'

When Amy looked into Luke's eyes she realised that work was his life because it *had* to be. He'd been on his own for ever. The only thing he knew was to get the job done on his own. Maybe working had served him well when things in his personal life had got rough. But that was in the past, and the past was over.

'What are you doing here, Luke?'

'I just have to get this finished. It won't take too much longer. I'm sorry, Amy. I'm not great company at the moment.'

'Don't you have people to do this for you? It's ten o'clock.'

'I *have* to get this finished.'

'I understand that, Luke. But that's not why you're here so late and not with me, is it?'

His brow furrowed.

'You're here because you don't want to deal with me. With *us*. You're using work as a way of not dealing with what's happening between us.'

'Amy...'

'No. Stop avoiding me. Don't do that again. Look

what happened the last time we stopped talking to each other.'

'Amy, it's just not simple…'

'No, it's *not* simple. Life gets complicated and sometimes you have to take a risk. *I'm* willing to take that risk, Luke, but are you?'

His eyes searched hers and his hands didn't leave her hips. Then he breathed in deeply. 'It's late, Amy, and I'm tired. I'm sorry that I didn't come and meet you. I lost track of time, that's all. I'm not avoiding you, or using work to not deal with anything. I just need to get this done.'

For some reason his speech made Amy sad. She'd wanted him to say yes, that he was willing to take the risk. She'd wanted him to say more. She wasn't sure what, but…*more*.

'I can see you thinking, Lolli. And worrying. Don't.' He pulled her in closer and her arms fell around his shoulders. 'Everything's fine. *We're* fine. I've got you. I just need to get this done.'

Amy wanted to shout and demand that he tell her he wanted her. She wanted him to explain why he was here and not with her. She wanted to know what the hell was going on. But he'd said 'we're fine', as if there actually was a 'we', so instead she just rubbed the back of her hand on the stubble that had formed on his cheek.

His face seemed so familiar to her now. So comfortable in such a short space of time. She knew every line and eyelash. She wanted answers, but she knew he wasn't going to give her any. Not tonight anyway.

He was distracted and stressed and instead of demanding the answers she desperately needed now all Amy wanted to do was help. She wanted to massage him, run her hands over the tight, worn muscles on his body—make him feel better.

'I tell you what—how about I help you with this? Then we can go back to the hotel and you can *show* me that everything's fine.'

His face broke out into a wide smile. 'I wish… But you can't help, Lolli. I've got to do this on my own.'

Amy's hand flew off his cheek and gripped his shirt—hard. His eyes opening wide in surprise.

'Do you have *any* idea who I am?' she asked, going for a sinister look on her face.

Luke raised an eyebrow in a fantastically sexy move that made Amy's body heat in the way only he could make it do.

'I am Bird Marketing's number one PR executive. I've negotiated deals and organised campaigns that have made millions of dollars. My skills are legendary and I'm here, practically sitting on your lap…' Luke shifted his legs and she moved in closer—so close her breasts were almost touching his chin. A violent shiver rolled up Amy's spine at the heat of him so close. 'I demand you take advantage of me.'

Heat shone in Luke's eyes as they shifted to her lips. His hands grabbed her hips violently and shoved her closer to him till the heat of his chest burned through her dress and right into her now throbbing core.

'I don't answer to demands.'

His teeth bit down on his bottom lip as he moved his head closer to her breast. She saw what he was planning, and her nipples ached to feel his mouth on them, but she pushed him back.

'Then we should negotiate.'

'I don't negotiate.'

She peered down at him, her eyebrow raised the same way as his, and she saw the same reaction in him as she'd felt. His hands skated up her back and pulled her in tighter, but again she pulled back.

He reconsidered. 'What would your opening offer be?'

She pretended to think as she held him back. She strained against him as his mouth sought her breasts. 'How about this? You spend at least an hour kissing my entire body and I'll help you with whatever's going on here. Then we go back to the hotel and I'll spend an hour kissing *your* entire body.'

He considered her for a second, before his mouth reached for her breasts. She had to push against him violently so he could not make contact. His face flushed and she knew what he wanted. She'd seen that look in his eyes so many times.

Amy reached down to lift the edge of her dress up over her knee, then shifted herself so she was sitting in his lap. She wanted to find a way to make him feel better…she wanted to help. First by relaxing his mind and then by seeing what she could do to make his job a little easier. Now she was perched on Luke's long legs her breasts were tantalisingly close to his mouth. She knew he was frantic by now—she could feel him hard beneath her. *This* was the help he needed right now. Physical release.

'Deal,' he said gruffly, and his lips met her neck with a violent, deep kiss.

Amy let out a satisfying moan as his hands pulled her in close. She couldn't hold him back any more. His mouth kissed up her neck to her mouth and his kiss was hard and demanding. She pulled away, breathless—her entire body pulsating with white-hot desire for him.

'You haven't really grasped the concept of negotiation, have you?'

He kissed her neck again, then slipped his thumb under the strap of her dress to lift her it off her shoulder. When it dropped her breast spilled free, and he hesitated for only a second before cupping it in his big hand and slipping her nipple into his mouth. Her head fell back. She moved her hips to feel him hard and strong against her.

'I've achieved the outcome I wanted,' he said, only lifting his mouth off for a second to answer her.

'You're easily pleased. But unfortunately for you, I'm not. My expectations for this deal are high, Mr Moore.'

'They will be exceeded, Miss McCarthy.'

She wanted to say, *We'll see*, but she didn't get a chance to. He lifted her up off the seat and had her back on the desk before she could speak. With one sweeping move her flimsy dress was over her head and all that lay between them was a very small item of underwear.

Amy fumbled at his belt buckle but he removed that for her too. His manic desire for her turned her on. The look in his eyes turned her on. The way they'd come to an agreement turned her on. She was gone. She knew that now. There was no turning back and no caution. She was his and he needed to know that.

Tonight there was no time for talking, but tomorrow—there would have to be. Because Amy could feel herself slipping into a feeling she knew she'd not be able to get herself out of.

'Off—it needs to be off.' She tugged at her underwear and he helped her remove it before climbing on top of her, his knees perched on the desk.

First he used his hands to stroke the length of her body. Not missing anything. Touching everywhere. He left a wake of trembling flesh, and Amy did what she'd learned to do with Luke—let go. There was no use trying to stay in control when she was with him and no use worrying.

She closed her eyes for a moment to enjoy his touch, then opened them. She wanted to see him watching her. She wanted to *know* him. When they were together like this there was no thinking or negotiating. They just *did*.

Using each other's sounds as a guide, they slid their way around each other's bodies, kissing and teasing and tasting until one or the other had had enough. This time it was Amy. She grabbed at his hips and moved them where she needed them to be. To where she was hot and swollen. She couldn't take another second without feeling him there.

She gasped when he entered her. No matter how many times she felt him inside her, it always surprised her. It wasn't just his size, it was the way he moved— as if he was hitting every spot she had, as if he knew exactly what she wanted. He thrust hard and she tried not to make a noise. She couldn't remember if she'd seen anyone else in the office, but with him moving like that she wasn't sure if she cared.

'Thank you for coming, Amy,' he whispered, letting his chest fall onto her.

'You're—' She gasped again as he raised himself up to thrust once more. 'Welcome!'

It came out as a moan and Luke smiled, knowing she was ready. The thrusting became deeper. Amy lifted her hips to meet him, her feet wrapped hard around his buttocks. She still wasn't sure if there was anyone else in the office but right now she didn't care. She had to cry out.

He gripped the back of her neck and lifted her up off the desk. His thrusts became purposeful and his face took on the angry, dirty look she knew so well. He was almost there, and Amy wanted to come with him.

Quickly she took his hand and let it slip between them. He knew what to do. His thumb circled her clitoris. First slowly, then more frantically and violently. Her orgasm grew. He felt her shake. He moved with her until her final scream pronounced her done, and as she shook he let himself tip over the edge as well, a deep, satisfied moan leaving his lips as she took everything he had to offer, cupped his chin with both hands and watched his mind clear of all his worries and be consumed by one thing. Her. Them. *Now.*

When Luke finally came to Amy was sitting on the desk in front of him, naked, with her hands still cupped around his chin. Her eyes glowed...gold rings around the brown. Her cheeks and chest were flushed and her once perfect hair was wild and forming a halo around her face. She was beautiful—and that was the problem.

Little Lollipop was no longer his sister's naughty friend—she was *his* naughty friend. A gorgeous, sexy woman who managed to make him forget himself whenever he was with her. Something he shouldn't do. He'd tried so hard in the last few years to be strong— for everyone. To take his business to the highest level, to keep the people he loved safe. But no matter how hard he tried bad things happened.

As he watched her lips form a satisfied smile he wondered what bad things would happen with *this* relationship...

'Feeling better?'

The words purred off her lips. Her face was so familiar to him now. He loved the way her lips smiled on just one side first, before forming a full smile. He smiled back—he couldn't help it—before kissing the tiny freckle that sat on her collarbone. He'd explored every inch of her body—dozens of times—but she'd surprised him tonight.

He knew he'd been neglecting her. He knew that he should have left the office earlier. But he'd wanted to make sure everything was taken care of. And in the back of his mind he knew she was right. He was avoiding her. Not because he didn't want to be with her but because he'd realised this afternoon how it would feel if he didn't have her.

Her silence and distance had been torture. When she'd finally spoken to him he hadn't been able to help rushing at her and making love to her. He'd been so relieved. And now, afterwards, when they were sitting together watching the lights he felt so comfortable. *Too* comfortable.

This whole thing had been a mistake. A delicious, exciting, magnificent mistake, but a mistake nonetheless.

'I'm feeling much better.'

His teeth connected with her shoulder. He wondered if she was cold. Picking up his shirt from the chair behind him, he wrapped it round her shoulders. She took it, letting her arms slip into the too big sleeves.

'Well, then, now we need to tick off the other part of our deal.'

Help. She wanted to help. But she couldn't help. There was too much to do and not enough time to do it. There was no way she'd be able to help.

'There's no need for that. How about this?' Luke wrapped his arms around her and held her close, hoping his warmth would soothe her. 'How about I get this taken care of and you go back to the hotel and order us some food? I'm starving after that, and if I know you I bet you are too.'

She pushed at his chest. Hard. Surprisingly hard. 'We had a deal.'

He knew that look in her eye. She was getting mad. He needed to calm her.

'I know that, but I need to take care of this…'

'No.' She crossed her arms. 'That wasn't the deal.'

'Amy—'

'Sit.'

She used a foot to push him and the back of his legs hit the chair. He landed on his ass with a thump.

'It's time you listened to me. We had a *deal*.'

Amy uncrossed her arms and stood over him, one arm either side of the chair. Her hair fell forward and her eyes narrowed. She was angry. And dead sexy. He resisted the urge to pull her onto his lap and kiss her. *Just.*

'And the deal was that we relax you, then fix whatever problem you have. Together. You and me. Not you on your own, taking on the responsibilities of the world. Not you on your own, thinking no one else can do this. I've come a long way since Weeping Reef, Luke. I've had to grow up. To manage people and figure things out. And I've figured *you* out.'

She turned her chair so the window was at her back. The lights of Singapore sparkled behind her and his shirt billowed out in front. It wasn't the lights he was looking at. It was her. Angry and determined and making him listen like no other woman ever had.

'You think the only way to stop bad things happening is by taking on all the responsibility. But life happens either way. You can't take on the responsibility for everyone. People make their own choices and they deal with the consequences. Your job is not to save them but to be there for them when they fall. Because they will. Everyone does at some point. I know. I fell once and you caught me.'

But he *hadn't* caught her, had he? He'd let that bad thing happen to her. And he'd let his sister marry the wrong man. And he hadn't been there for Koko. He knew Amy was just trying to help, to make him feel better. And he liked her for that. Other women would have walked away when he neglected them, but not Amy. She'd tracked him down, sat him down and made him accountable. That was what he needed. Someone who saw his darkness and liked him anyway.

With a gentle kiss he let her know that he appreciated her and her lecture and that slow little smile of hers crept over her face.

'Good. Let's get started. What's the name of that witch making your life hell?'

'Kel Huynh.'

'I'll start with her.'

Amy *had* changed from her Weeping Reef days. There was still a lot of fun and cheeky jokes, but there was no wandering off and getting distracted, no trying to get out of what she was supposed to be doing. She was all business.

She pulled out all the paperwork he needed. She read through his to-do list and suggested ways to delegate. He didn't agree with all her suggestions—

after all, she couldn't know the ins and outs of this project and who would be able to handle it and who wouldn't—but she had a way of convincing him to try it her way.

Her salesmanship was magnificent. She complimented, joked, dropped little-known facts, used distraction—all the tricks in the book. But mostly she flirted, and *that* was when he couldn't resist. Amy in full flirt was like nothing he'd ever seen. She knew just how to tilt her head and play with her hair and smile and bat her eyelashes. She knew just what to say—innocent with a slightly shocking twist—as if she knew exactly what she was talking about. Which she did.

Amy was an expert. She knew how to get what she wanted—she always had. But he didn't mind her using her charms on him. He liked her charms. Especially when her charms were dressed in just his shirt. Watching her breasts peep out from where she'd loosely buttoned the shirt made all thoughts fly from his head. He'd do whatever she wanted and she knew it. He had to fight to stay in control. He had to fight to stop himself from grabbing her and kissing her every five seconds.

'All done, I think.'

She smiled as she punched the last of his data into the spreadsheet. He watched her from where he stood, next to where she was sitting. He watched her fingers fly over the keyboard. She didn't look at them—just kept her eyes on the screen.

Amy had always been a quick learner. When

they'd changed the computer system on Weeping Reef a month after she'd started she'd been the first in the office to master it. He remembered the time she'd spent at the others' desks, showing them what to do. At the time he'd been frustrated. She'd been neglecting her own work. She hadn't got things done. But now he realised how lucky he'd been to have her. He hadn't had the time to show the staff the new system. She'd been doing him a favour by taking their questions and explaining things to them.

He hadn't appreciated her back then. In his head she'd always just been his sister's silly friend who talked too much and didn't get her work done on time. He wished he'd seen her then as he did now. He wished he'd noticed how generous and caring she was instead of focussing on himself and what needed to be done. Maybe she would never have had to go through with what she had if he'd taken more notice of her. Taken the time to get to know her. Listened to her.

Luke moved closer and slipped his hand across her shoulder. She stopped to put a hand over his and smile at him. But he didn't smile back. He couldn't when all he could think about was that she deserved more. So much more than he could give.

'You're amazing—you know that?'

She smiled and dimples embedded themselves in her cheeks. 'About time you realised that.'

It was. About time.

When they'd finally packed up and gone back to the hotel she decided he needed to watch her slowly undress before she climbed on top of him and made each and every one of his thoughts disappear from his head. And he found himself wondering again why the hell he hadn't realised how amazing she was eight years ago.

CHAPTER THIRTEEN

WHEN AMY SAID she had a surprise for him the next morning he was hoping it involved more nakedness, but she was dressed and standing in his office—he'd managed to convince her to let him go there for a few hours.

'Time to go,' she said firmly, her eyes connecting with his.

He knew there was no use arguing. And with her help yesterday some of the pressure had actually been relieved. He'd delegated some of the less pressing tasks and managed to get everything together and now it would be on the desk of the demanding Ms Huynh.

There was nothing left to do but wait. And enjoy the delights of Singapore. With Amy.

'Back to the hotel?' he asked hopefully, getting up to put his arms around her waist and kissing her hard on the lips.

She twisted her arms around his neck and pressed herself closer. Her breasts pushed against his chest and he hardened instantly. No one had ever turned him on more that Amy, although a niggling fear had bored itself into his brain like a spider and taken up residence there. Pressing on his nerves whenever he started to think things he shouldn't. Like this might last. Like this was something important. Like he never wanted to let her go.

'No...' she murmured between kisses.

He liked it that she couldn't get enough of him either. He enjoyed the way she became breathless and a little vague every time they kissed. As if kissing him made her forget everything the way kissing her did him.

'No. Not back to the hotel. Somewhere better.'

She smiled that slow smile of hers and his heart clamped. She was an amazing flirt. He had to remember that and not take all this too seriously. It had only been a few weeks that she'd been back in his life—it was moving quickly. Too quickly. He needed to slow this down. Stay in control. Keep his eye and his damn heart steady so everything stayed where it should be.

'Nowhere could be better than the hotel with you.'

Luke let his hands slide up her back under the white shirt she was wearing. Her skin was soft and smooth and he wanted to kiss it. Kiss her everywhere. Sex would help him forget what he was worrying about and it would mean she couldn't ask any more questions he didn't want to answer.

'Trust me—you're going to love it.'

'Surprises weren't part of our deal.'

'No, they weren't, but this is not negotiable. You've

flown me all the way here and I want to see some of Singapore.'

'We're not going on one of those awful double-decker buses, are we?'

'Don't worry—you'll enjoy it.'

'As long as you're there I will.'

Her eyes met his for too long. He had to remember not to say things like that. That type of thing sounded a little too 'relationshippy', and he didn't want her to think that that was what this was. Not that Amy wasn't someone he could see himself having a relationship with—if there was anyone he'd want to spend every day with it would be her—but he was better at taking care of people from a distance.

'That sounded as if you're starting to like having me around, Luke Moore.' She smiled breezily. 'Tell me the truth: is it my devastatingly awesome PR and management skills that turn you on so much?'

No. It was the way she teased him and never let him take himself too seriously. And the way she worried about him when he worked too hard. And the way she knew exactly what he needed. And the way her body seemed to fit so perfectly with his. There were a million reasons he liked having her around and only one reason why he couldn't. He'd already let her down once. He'd let something bad happen to her and that had changed her. He couldn't be responsible for someone like Amy.

'That must be it.'

'Or maybe you're starting to realise what a catch I am?'

'You *are* a catch, Amy. You're gorgeous and smart and funny and I've never seen anyone work a spreadsheet quite like you. You'll make some lucky man very happy one day.'

Her expression froze for just a second. But then she smiled and the hesitation in her eyes was gone. Perhaps he'd just imagined it.

'We should go,' she said brightly.

For a moment he thought about the man who would eventually marry Amy and a wave of hot jealousy rolled over his body. Amy needed someone reliable. Someone she could depend on. Someone who didn't make her angry like he did. Someone who wouldn't let her down as he once had.

She chatted breezily as they went downstairs to get a taxi. She mentioned that Willa had called earlier that day and had wanted to tell her some news but had been called away. His sister had a habit of making spontaneous decisions—like the one she'd made when she got married. That had ended in disaster. He wondered what scheme she was coming up with now. Of *course* she'd call Amy about her crazy plans. The two were thick as thieves. Even thicker now than they had been at the resort all those years ago. Which was another reason a relationship with Amy wasn't a good idea. It would become awkward…it was all too close.

Luke glanced at Amy in the cab. It was a typically hot Singaporean day. Amy's hair wasn't as blow-dried and straight over here as it was back home in Australia. The humidity gave it a kink and it looked a little like the way she'd used to wear it back on the reef.

Only then her hair had been longer, and usually dripping in jewellery and leather straps and gemstones. And back then she'd usually worn a lot less.

She'd become rather conservative over the eight years when he hadn't seen her. In Sydney she mostly wore suits, but over the last couple of days the old Amy had begun to emerge. Today she had on a top that exposed her belly and some very short shorts. And instead of a bra he could see a bikini top tied around her neck. He liked it. He liked the bohemian she hid beneath her corporate slick. He knew who she really was. Troublemaker Amy, with a definite thirst for adventure and fun.

So opposite to him. He had responsibilities, and he needed to be the reliable, dependable man he'd been working hard to be—and yet he couldn't help admiring the way Amy didn't let her own responsibilities stop her from living life. Not that he'd ever be able to live like that.

He slipped his fingers through hers and held on tight. She smiled and shifted a little closer and he liked her there. Close and warm and completely his… at least until life and work inevitably got in the way. But he didn't want to think about that. Not today. The sun was out and there was a beautiful woman wanting to make him happy. Today the only thing he wanted to think about was Amy.

Amy had slipped the cab driver a piece of paper with the address of where they were going on it, so he still had no idea where they were headed, but when they passed the huge sign signalling the entrance to Sentosa Beach he started to wonder.

'The beach? You want to go to the *beach*? There are possibly five hundred better beaches in Australia than this, you know.'

'Not the beach.' She smiled and squeezed his hand.

'Then where…?'

The taxi sped past the manmade beach and the amusement park that was so popular with families and tourists and continued on.

'The *wharf*?'

'Yep. The wharf. I've chartered a boat. And I've wiped your schedule. Today I have you all to myself, with no mobile connection. We have champagne and food and paddleboards and that's it.'

It sounded like the perfect day to Luke—but no mobile connection…? 'What if Kel Huynh needs me?'

'She'll have to wait.'

Amy sidled even closer and rested her head on his shoulder. They couldn't go on for much longer like this. It was impossible. But a day out on a yacht with Amy for company sounded so good that for now he just wanted to enjoy it.

Amy smiled at Rocky, the captain of the yacht she'd chartered with a little help from the concierge at the hotel. He'd given them the safety speech and was now firing up the engine. Luke had volunteered to uncork the champagne, so Amy had come to the front of the boat to enjoy the views that were whizzing past her as they headed for one of the small islands that lay around Singapore.

The sun was warm, but not too hot. Unlike in Australia, there were no flies here—the humidity was horrendous for her hair, but somehow that just made it feel more like a holiday.

Amy stood with her back to the window of the cabin. She breathed in deeply and the salt air filled her lungs. She was happy, and it was a strange kind of happiness. Something she'd never felt before. A kind of dozy, lazy happiness in which she was completely conscious of all the problems in her life but it was as if there was some strange drug running through her veins, making those problems seem so much more insignificant than they had just a few short weeks ago.

'Here we go.'

Luke passed her a champagne glass. He'd opted for a beer, and Amy loved that about him. He was honest and real. He clearly didn't like champagne, but rather than drink it and say nothing, as Laurie would have done, he'd got himself a beer and done what he wanted.

Amy slipped a hand in his and moved close to him. He put his arm around her and for a moment everything was perfect. She wasn't sure if it would last, or if this would all end in tears, but right now it didn't matter.

The boat tipped and water sprayed up to cool them down as it sped out to sea. A few other boats were speeding past and the people on them waved as they caught their rip.

Luke leaned down to talk in her ear over the roar of the engine. 'I have to admit, Lolli…'

Amy smiled, the sound of his voice making her want to get naked right there. No one had ever done that to her. Luke had awakened some kind of sexual sprite in her and she was loving it. She loved trusting someone with her body. That had been taken away from her years ago, but with Luke's help it was back.

She slipped a hand up in between his shirt and his skin. He pulled her closer. He felt it as much as she did. She knew he couldn't get enough of her. He seemed to want to rip her clothes off every time they were alone…and sometimes when they weren't. His desire for her made her feel powerful and strong—something she hadn't felt in a long time.

Luke was healing her in a way Laurie never had. He made her angry and sad and happy and so turned on she couldn't bear it. Luke was bringing her back to life when Laurie had allowed her to sleep. He was giving her the strength to enjoy the life she'd left home for. He was making her finally think that making the move from Melbourne had been a good one.

But something niggled at her still. The way he always put his work first. The way he could neglect her. It screamed of the old Luke. Closed and cold. And earlier he'd said she'd make someone a lucky man one day. But not him. That thought irritated her. What did he mean? Did that mean he thought they were going nowhere?

Amy's thoughts rattled in her head, getting mixed up and confused, and she shook her head. She couldn't think like that. She couldn't start reading into things and thinking about things that way. He'd probably meant nothing. She just wanted to feel happy—like she was now. She wanted to trust her feelings for once. She wanted to trust *him*. She wanted this to be real and she wanted it to last. It had to last because… because this was different. It wasn't safe. It wasn't predictable and it wasn't one-sided.

She could see that Luke cared for her in the way he looked at her when he thought she didn't notice, and the way he touched her, and the way he was constantly trying to protect her. And she cared about him too. A lot. She…she *loved* him.

Amy tried to shake herself back into the moment. As she looked across at Luke he grinned at her. He had mirrored sunglasses on, so when she looked at him all she saw was her own reflection. A pair of trusting brown eyes staring at him. Even she could see the pathetic puppy dog love in them.

She smiled and took a deep breath. It was okay. He had her. He'd had her back at Weeping Reef. When the absolute worst had happened it had been Luke who'd had her and he had her now. Yesterday, when they'd had that fight and she'd thought she'd lost him, he'd assured her that he had her and it had made her feel safe and out of control all at once—and she'd liked it. The feeling was addictive and she wasn't ready to let it go yet.

'I have to admit this was a pretty good idea,' he said, leaning down again.

'I only have good ideas.'

'That's true. You're with me, aren't you?'

Her grin was wide. 'Perhaps that was *not* one of my best ideas. But I'm a glass half-full kinda girl—I can make the best of any situation. I'm sure I can work with you,' she teased.

He took the bait. She could always rely on him to. He *got* her.

'You can work with me, can you? Tell me, Lolli, what would you change about me if you could?'

His smile was wide and it showed off the tan he was starting to acquire since coming home to Australia and not working as much, spending more time outdoors. Sunshine and fun agreed with him.

She considered her answer. What would she change? Nothing. Except for his overbearing need to take care of everyone and be so responsible all the time. But she even liked that about him. As annoying as it was, you knew when Luke Moore cared about you because he didn't let you out of his sight.

'I'd change that belt. Black belt and brown shoes? *So* not working.'

He chuckled and looked down at his outfit. He was wearing his usual work attire today, *sans* the jacket, but she'd thought of that and packed him a pair of board shorts down in the cabin. She'd bring them out when they anchored. Seeing his gorgeous body in a pair of low slung boardies was going to be one of the highlights of the day.

'Besides my apparently appalling taste in fashion, of course.'

'Besides that?' She considered him, then raised her

hand to lift his sunnies. She wanted to see his eyes. He pushed them to the top of his head and she studied him. From the wrinkles at the sides of his eyes to his stubble-covered jaw. 'Nothing.'

He breathed deeply and something changed between them. Something crackled to life that hadn't been there before.

'And that's what I'd change about you too. Nothing.'

'We must be perfect.'

'We must be.'

Their conversation was simple. And Amy liked it. It made her feel that maybe she was right. Maybe she *should* love him. Maybe this was actually real.

His eyes locked with hers and he brought his arms down to encircle her waist, keeping her tight against him and still. Slowly, carefully, he bent his head and kissed her. Amy felt the bones in her body disappear. She leaned into him. This wasn't one of his usual manic, sexually charged kisses. Although it was still damn sexy. This was slower, deeper. He was taking his time and creating a soothing, slow rhythm with his tongue.

She responded, holding him tightly around his neck and communicating with him the way he was with her. She knew it now. He loved her back. No one could kiss someone like that and not love them.

They stood for too many minutes, kissing and being totally unaware of what was going on around them. Amy wasn't sure how long they kissed, but when they stopped she was out of breath and so was he. He looked as if he was about to say something, but at that moment Rocky appeared and they realised the boat had stopped.

Rocky coughed awkwardly. 'I just need to get in here and release the anchor rope.'

They moved aside and shared a grin as Rocky anchored before disappearing back down to the cabin.

'I think that means it's time for swimming. You wait there.'

Amy's heart was so full she was scared it would burst. After that kiss there could be nothing else for him to say but that he loved her. She wanted to hear it. She wanted to feel the words wash over her. She realised it had been for eight long years she'd wanted him to feel this way about her, and today it was going to happen.

Grabbing the board shorts, she headed back up, her heart pounding. When she saw him smiling at her, her hands shook. She wanted to hear him say it, so why was she so anxious now?

'Here you go—I packed these. I didn't think you'd have boardies on underneath that suit. You can get changed—or do you want to go down to the cabin? There are a few boats about—maybe you want to go down?'

She was rambling. Her words were coming out too quickly. She tried to think of more. What was she *doing*? It was as if she didn't want him to get a word in. As if she didn't want him to say the words she was longing to hear. What was *wrong* with her? Of course she did. She wanted him to feel that way about her. She wanted to know. What the hell was she so scared of?

His brow furrowed. 'You okay, Amy?'

She nodded. 'Of course—perfect. I think I just need more champagne. I'll go get some. Unless you want to get changed first? Or we could go together? There's plenty of room down there. You'd have your privacy. I mean, if you need it.'

His arms were around her in a second. 'Amy. You've seen me naked plenty of times. I don't think it matters if you see me get changed.'

'Yeah—yes. Of course.' Her laugh was forced. Nervous. What the hell was going on with her? 'So we should…go…together.'

'We should.'

He laughed, taking the board shorts from her and holding her hand before leading her to the back of the boat and the cabin below.

Rocky passed them in the doorway on his way out. 'So I'll leave you two for a couple of hours and come back?'

They watched as he boarded a paddleboard and headed towards the shore. Amy watched him go and the fluttering in her belly started to grow. *Come back now!* she felt like screaming. For the first time since she'd seen Luke on that chair at Saints she was frightened to be alone with him. What the hell for?

'All alone…what should we do now?'

There was no mistaking the look in his eye. She knew what he wanted. She wanted it too. As she watched him peel off his shirt she wanted it so badly.

But after they were done he would probably say what he was going to say, and she wasn't sure she was ready for that. Not yet. First they should do some paddleboarding. Yes—that was what they should do.

'You get changed and I'll get the paddleboards ready.' She fled before he could argue.

When he emerged, gorgeously tanned, his muscled torso was begging to be touched. But she didn't touch him. She handed him a paddle.

'You're really keen for this paddleboarding thing, then?' he teased, taking the paddle and playfully smacking her behind with it.

Amy turned away. She needed to think. She had to figure out what the hell she was scared of right now—and watching him there, half naked and teasing her, wasn't helping.

Amy pulled off her clothes and pushed a paddleboard out into the ocean, before diving in and emerging to haul herself up on it. Within minutes she'd mastered the oar and was paddling fast—away from the boat, away from Luke, and away from the conversation she wanted to have but which scared the hell out of her.

A half-hour later Amy's arms were burning. Her thighs were sore and she could feel the burn of the sun on her shoulders.

'You're doing it wrong.'

Luke appeared like a shark in the water and tilted her board. Amy faltered but kept her balance. He laughed and she growled.

'You've gotta be a little more stealthy than that to

fool me, Moore.' She poked at him with the oar and he disappeared under the blue-green water—only to appear on the other side.

'What are you doing out here all alone? I thought you wanted to entertain me?'

He shook the board again but she stood steady, still swiping at him from her position up high.

'I never said I was here to entertain you.'

'Then what *are* we here for?'

Amy steadied herself and glared at Luke, whose hands were wrapped ominously around her board, and sat down, one leg either side of the board.

'I wanted to sightsee.'

'The only sight you need to see is me.'

Amy let out a little gasp and an embarrassingly girly squeal as Luke pushed on the board.

'Permission to climb aboard, Captain?'

'No! Permission not granted. Stop! We'll both fall!'

The board rocked dangerously but Luke kept coming, sliding his stomach onto the board before swinging a leg over. He grabbed her shoulders and held her steady as she tried to keep still.

'No, we won't. I've got you, Amy.'

'No, you haven't!' She grabbed at him, desperately trying to stay upright.

'Stop moving, Amy. I've *got* you. Hold still.'

His deep voice reverberated through her head and she listened to him. He had her. All she had to do was be still. Amy breathed in deep and looked at his face, his smiling lips and his eyes. He had her. She just needed to stop.

'There. What did I tell you? You need to learn to trust me, Lollipop.'

He grinned, and she grinned back. Trust. That was what they had. That was what she'd never had. Not since that night at Weeping Reef. Not really. That jerk had taken away all her trust, and even though Laurie had helped she knew she still kept a thick wall up.

She hid it well. Behind the non-stop working and the late-night parties and the quick jokes and the perfect outfits. But Luke had managed to get behind her wall. She was here, with limp, frizzy hair, in a vulnerable position, and he had her. Why had she been avoiding him? He *had* her. He'd had her eight years ago and he had her now.

Luke was facing her, one leg either side of the board, and she shifted so she was a little closer. Then she placed her hands on the board in front of her and carefully, while trying to maintain her balance, pushed herself towards him. His eyes darkened. His grin disappeared. He made a deep noise in the back of his throat before leaning forward and meeting her lips.

Their kiss was fast and furious and gained desperation as time wore on. He shifted closer and she did the same, all the while clamping her thighs around the board.

'That's better,' he muttered. 'Nice and close— that's where I want you.'

'That's where I want *you*.'

He smiled beneath the kiss. 'Yeah, right—until you

have another party to go to. I know you, Amy. You're a wild animal. Can never be tied down or tamed.'

She smiled back. 'Maybe not, but there's something to be said for staying wild.'

'There is?'

He spoke between kisses and Amy's body heated. She wanted him. Right here, on this board, in the ocean, with an audience of at least fifteen boats full of people around them. This was what he did to her. He made her feel as if no one and nothing else existed. Just him and her.

'Of course there is. Domesticated animals get fat and lazy and scared, and they depend on their owners for everything. That's not a life. Wild and free—that's a life.'

Luke leaned back, stopping the kiss. Amy missed it. She wanted to taste more of him. She leaned forward again but he hesitated.

'There's something to be said about domestication too, you know,' he said.

'Is there? I can't think of anything.'

His brow furrowed. 'That animal knows where his next meal is coming from. He knows he has a safe home to come to at the end of the night. He has a family who take care of him.'

'Maybe. But where's the fun in *that*?'

Amy was keeping it light and cute. She wanted him to kiss her again. But whatever she was saying wasn't working. He didn't lean forward again.

'So what you're saying is…you want a cat?'

'No.' He smiled. 'No. I don't want a cat. I want a tiger.'

Then he leaned forward and kissed her so hard and so fast that any chance of balance completely left her and they toppled together into the ocean.

Water went up Amy's nose and she emerged spluttering and laughing, her eyes stinging from the salt. But she wasn't alone long, because Luke had his arms around her and was kissing her again.

'I forgot—tigers can't swim!'

Amy laughed and pushed on his chest. '*This* tiger can.'

And she left him smiling as she cut long, smooth strokes through the water. Her time on Weeping Reef hadn't been completely wasted. One thing she could definitely do well now was swim. She'd spent every morning on the island in the resort pool, and even after all this time she was so fast Luke didn't catch her until they were back at the boat.

As they climbed Amy playfully pushed him back in, and when she laughed and offered him a hand he pulled her back into the water. She knew she looked like a drenched rat. She had no make-up left and her hair was plastered over her face. But she didn't care. He didn't care. And she knew. She was in love with Luke and he was in love with her and she was finally ready to hear it.

'You go on up top,' Luke insisted when they finally managed to get on board. 'I'll get us some food and drinks. You dry off.'

She smiled, wanting to kiss him and wanting to

punch him as well. Of *course* she wanted him to say he loved her. Her apprehension had nothing to do with him and everything to do with her. She'd been a good girlfriend to Laurie for years. She'd been faithful and loyal and just as loving to him as he had been to her. But then she'd changed. What she wanted had changed. That didn't mean she was bad and didn't deserve love.

Luke had made her feel that she did. With Laurie, sex had been slow and respectful. With Luke anything went. Luke had been the one to save her from the attack on the island. He'd helped her then and soothed her, made her feel that what had happened hadn't been her fault, and he was doing the same thing now. She loved him for that. And she deserved the love he was offering in return.

Lying back on the deck, with the ocean below, Amy started to relax. This had always been meant to happen. She'd been meant to have this break from Luke. In order to grow up. In order to gain some perspective. And they were meant to meet now. It was right. It was time. And she was ready.

Luke didn't take long with the food and drinks and their former comfortableness returned as they teased each other and fed each other and laughed and played on the deck of the boat. When they'd finished Luke rubbed sunscreen into her already red shoulders and back, and she did the same for him.

She lay on his lap, her face turned towards the sun, and they just sat—full and content and not needing to talk for a long time.

'This has been just what I needed, Amy. How do you *do* that?'

'What?'

'Know exactly what I need?'

'I'm your soul mate—that's how.'

The words fell out before she could stop them. Her heart lay heavy and her breathing stopped.

Luke was silent, and a tingling caution crept over Amy.

'Do you believe in soul mates, Luke?'

For a long time he didn't answer. Her nervousness returned. She couldn't help but notice his hesitation.

'I don't know about that, Amy. You meet people, they teach you things—and then they leave. That's normally how it works.'

'Not everyone leaves.' Fear edged her nervousness. What was he saying?

'Everyone leaves.' His voice was quiet.

'Even you?' She wasn't looking at him. She was talking into the breeze. She couldn't face him.

'Even me.'

The world stopped turning. Amy's heart stopped beating. A primal instinct she hadn't known she had roared within her. Slowly turning, she faced him, sitting up.

'Luke…' She tried to smile. 'You don't mean that.'

His hands were behind him, he looked relaxed and casual, but he took off his sunglasses and met her eyes. 'I'm not a keeper, Amy. We both know that.'

'What does that mean?'

Amy's heart beat faster. This wasn't what he was

supposed to say. *I love you. I need you. I can't live without you.* Not this.

'You know what it means. You know what I'm like.'

'No. Tell me. What *are* you like?'

'Married to my work. Absent. Unreliable.'

Amy's brow furrowed and breathing became difficult. What was he trying to say?

'You're a hard worker. So am I. That doesn't mean you can't have a relationship.'

'No, it doesn't. But the person I have a relationship with would have to be very understanding. And forgiving. Nothing like *you*.'

He laughed, and her fear and nervousness gave way to something else. Anger.

'Nothing like me? Oh? Why? Because I'm a wild animal? A thoughtless, silly party girl? Because I can't be serious? Because what you want is someone more *domesticated*?'

'No...'

'Or is it because I can't hold down a relationship? Because I change my mind? Because I put myself first? I told you about Laurie the other night because I thought you'd understand—not because I thought you'd hold it against me.'

'That's not what I meant, Amy. I just meant that you need someone who can take care of you. Who knows how to handle you. Who can protect you.'

Amy stood up over him. 'I don't need a keeper. I need a partner. Which is what I thought you wanted to be for me. I guess I was wrong.'

Why had she said that about soul mates? This wasn't how the conversation was supposed to go. He was supposed to be saying he loved her, but he wasn't doing it. He was making her heart hurt. Why had she said that...? But then again, what if she hadn't?

Luke stood too now, and towered over her. But she wasn't afraid. She deserved love. Luke had taught her that. She wanted him and they were supposed to be together—she knew that now. She'd found herself in these past few weeks. She'd realised that what she wanted wasn't wrong. He'd helped her find that out and he wasn't getting out of it that easily. She knew he loved her—she'd felt it. So why was he saying this?

'You need someone to take care of you.'

'No, I don't. I need you.'

Luke stared at her. He didn't move. She could see his mind ticking but he still didn't speak. And then he just turned and left her standing alone in the bow of the boat. Angry, confused and hurt.

What the hell had just happened?

No. He wasn't doing this. He wasn't going to shut her out. Not after the last three weeks. Not after this perfect day. And not after she'd finally realised what she was looking for. *Him.*

'Don't walk away, Luke. We need to talk about this. About us. About what's happening here.'

Luke didn't answer. He just kept walking until he got to the cabin and pulled another beer out of the fridge.

'Luke...'

'I shouldn't be here. You know Kel Huynh is getting back to me today and yet you drag me out here.'

Luke picked up his phone and moved it in the air.

'Luke, forget work. We need to talk about *this*.'

'Forget work? Do you know who I *am*, Amy? Do you know what I *do*? You say you work hard, but you don't have a business to run. You don't have a family to take care of. What about Willa? You said she called—maybe something's wrong? I haven't spoken to my father since I came back to Sydney, and this project will fall over if I don't sort all this out. Don't you understand? I don't have time to be out here on a boat, rubbing suntan lotion into your back and talking about our feelings. I have *work* to do. You know— like a responsible adult. I'm not an overgrown party animal, Amy. I'm not wild and free like you. I'm domesticated and I *like* being domesticated. People rely on me. They need me. And while you're around I'm letting everyone else down.'

His speech ended in silence. Luke didn't even know what he'd said in the end. He'd just been talking, moving his lips. Distracting her. Distracting himself.

He'd felt something earlier. In that kiss he hadn't been able to break away from. A dangerous connection that had felt so right and so bloody wrong at the same time. He couldn't do this. He needed to get back to work. He couldn't look at her face for one more minute because he'd let her down again. Maybe not today, maybe not tomorrow, but eventually. And he couldn't face that.

He checked his phone. No reception. No connection. All he had to look at was her disappointment and hurt. Just as he had that night, all those years ago. A man had taken from her what hadn't been his to take.

He'd found that man that night, and he'd made him sorry he'd ever come to Weeping Reef. Then he'd packed the bastard up and sent him away. Banned him for life from that resort and any other resort Luke had ever worked at. Now he was the one who needed to be exiled.

Without another word he went to the boat's radio and contacted Rocky, and within ten minutes they were heading back to the city. Back to real life and not this fantasy world where anything could happen. Where Amy could actually be his. She thought it would work out because she was young and hopeful and optimistic, but he knew what would happen. He'd never be able to give her what she truly deserved from a relationship—not long-term.

When the boat docked Amy was off and onto dry land in seconds. She didn't say goodbye. She hadn't said anything since his outburst and he didn't blame her. But this was the right thing to do. They couldn't fool themselves and think this might be something it never would be. Better she knew that now rather than five years down the track, when they were married and had a couple of kids.

He watched her go, her legs moving fast and her arms folded tightly across her chest. He didn't stop her. Why would he? What would he say that he hadn't said already? The best thing now was to let her go and hope that one day she would find someone she could rely on. Someone who could prevent bad things happening from her.

His phone beeped manically. Twenty-five messages. He needed to get back to work. He needed to focus. He had to get back to reality and not think about the wild animal that was now running as far away from him as she could.

Amy felt a kick on the back of her seat for the eleventh time. They hadn't even taken off. She should be in first class right now. Enjoying a relaxing glass of champagne and sharing a blanket with Luke. But she couldn't sit next to him. She couldn't even look at him.

As soon as she'd got back to the hotel she'd gone to Reception and got another room. She'd expected him to call or message her but he hadn't. Not once. Not even to check that she was all right. He didn't care. He never had. That thought made her feel the same way it had the last two hundred times she'd thought it. Sick.

The thumping behind her began again. Then came the crying and the calling out. 'Mummy!'

Amy stuck in her earplugs and closed her eyes. She tried to stop the tears in her eyes from falling but she couldn't, so she put on an eye mask and cried for eight hours straight.

When she landed back in Sydney she told herself to stop.

'Enough.'

Her phone beeped insistently as soon as she'd picked up her luggage. Ten missed calls. Two from work and eight from Willa. She dialled her friend's number immediately. She hadn't called Willa back about her news. She didn't want to speak to anyone but it was time now.

'Amy! You're back! Yay! Yay!'

Willa was smiling. Amy could feel it through the phone.

'I'm back.' Amy tried to smile too. *Enough,* she told herself again.

'I've been trying to get hold of you for two days. What's been happening—how's Luke?'

Amy hadn't told Willa about her relationship with Luke. She'd told her friend she was going with him to Singapore to research his hotel business for her own work. She was sure Willa hadn't bought it, but—as the good friend she was—she'd pretended to.

'Fine. I think. What's happening with you—why have you been so desperate to get hold of me?'

'Oh, Amy. I have news and I needed you to know first! But I couldn't get hold of you—and I had to organise the party—it's this Saturday. We wanted to get everyone together while they're still in town!'

'Slow down, Wills. What party? What are you talking about?'

Willa laughed a joyful, happy laugh that made Amy's heart ache just a little bit.

'We're engaged, Amy! Rob and I are getting married!'

Of course they were. Perfect. Just what she wanted to hear after a disastrous break-up with the man she loved—the man she'd always loved. Possibly the only man she'd ever love.

Amy smiled as wide as she could. 'Willa, that's amazing news—congratulations!'

She really was happy for her friend. Willa had been through so much, and for her to find love again was wonderful. Amy thought perhaps she was being a little greedy, finding two men to love and marry within eight years…but that was irrelevant. She was over the moon that her friend was happy. But the news still made her chest ache and her stomach heavy.

Willa didn't seem to notice. Nor did she notice Amy's apprehension when she told her about the party on Saturday night. Luke would be there. She'd have to face him. See him and still be in love with him, knowing all the time that he didn't love her. That he'd put his responsibilities and his work before her. That he didn't consider her relationship potential because she was too 'wild'.

It was stupid and irrational, and a ridiculous reason not to love someone, but she couldn't help feeling hurt all the same. Because she wanted him to love her. So much. And she missed him already. The feel of his skin, the scent of his neck and the taste of his kisses. She needed him right now. With his big arms around her. Holding her up. Saving her as he always did.

But he wasn't there and he never would be. And on Saturday night she'd have to smile and act happy and pretend everything was okay. This was going to be the performance of her life.

CHAPTER FOURTEEN

AMY HAD BARELY had time to think about anything since she'd arrived back in Sydney on Monday. Her work had become manic and Willa had been calling her non-stop.

Amy was glad of it. The only time she cried now was when she was in the shower, and that didn't count because the tears might have been water and no one would know except for her puffy eyes the next day. Which she excused away with claims of jet lag and tiredness after a big weekend.

And yesterday she'd managed to go a whole hour without thinking of Luke. She'd been trying on dresses with Willa, and seeing her friend so in love had made her thoughts veer to him, but once her friend had started talking about how happy she was, and they'd begun trying on shoes and jewellery, talking about the new home Willa and Rob were going to build, Willa's excitement had taken over and Amy had felt genuinely happy. No pretending.

It had been a nice feeling, and she wanted to feel

that way again, but now the party was starting and she was hot. A storm was brewing over the humid city.

The party was being held at a harbourside restaurant. Willa had recently sold the harbourside mansion she'd shared with her ex-husband and was now living in an apartment that was way too small for the hundred or so people now mingling in the restaurant.

Cracks of lightning lit the starless sky and Amy counted the seconds before the boom of thunder. Ten seconds. Which meant the storm was ten kilometres away. Depending on which way the wind was blowing, they could expect rain in less than an hour. Torrential rain, by the look of the dark clouds that had rolled in and which now blanketed everything in a surreal darkness.

It was sticky and hot and uncomfortable, and the air was filled with a weird sort of apprehension. Which made her feel as if she wasn't the only one in the city tonight feeling sad.

She hadn't spotted Luke yet, and even though she told herself she didn't want to she knew she was dying to see his face again and watch him—see if he was happy, or miserable like her. He hadn't called. He hadn't made any contact. That was ripping at her inside, but she had to smile and get on with things. She couldn't change how he felt. All she could do was power through this tough time and hopefully come out not too scarred at the end.

Yeah, right, she scolded herself. The scars were going to be thick and deep with this one. She knew that already.

'Hey, Amy, thanks for helping this week. Willa's been a bit crazy. She settled down once you came home, though.'

It was Rob, Willa's soon-to-be husband. Amy liked Rob. He was calm and strong and he loved Willa fiercely. She wanted that for her friend. Everyone deserved to be loved like that. And it didn't hurt that he was handsome as all get-out.

'I've been happy to do it. I needed the distraction.'

'Distraction from what?'

Willa appeared, her hair pulled back in an elegant chignon and dressed in a gorgeous cream designer dress that made her pale skin glow.

'Ah…work…mostly.'

'Liar.'

That was the thing about best friends—you had to keep the good ones for life: they knew too much.

'I'm not lying. I've been busy since I got back—seems they can't operate without me…'

'Liar,' Willa repeated. 'Rob, could you go get me a drink?' She smiled sweetly at her fiancé.

'Of course—female code for, *Go away. We're about to have a deep and meaningful and you're not invited.*'

'That's why I love you, darling—you're so smart.'

Willa smiled and kissed her fiancé. Amy turned away.

'Now, Miss I'm-Going-to-Singapore-for-Research, are you going to tell me what the hell is going on between you and my brother or am I going to have to beat it out of you?'

She knew. Of course she knew. It was obvious.
Willa had known about Amy's crush on her brother
all those years ago and Willa had seen their connection in the bar that first night. Willa also knew that
Amy could sell snow to the Eskimos, but she couldn't
lie to her best friend.

'Nothing. Absolutely nothing. He's moved on.'

'Has he? Is that why he hasn't stopped growling at
me since you two got back? Is that why he's spending the night out on the balcony, arguing with anyone who walks past about how Australia was robbed
in the cricket?'

'Willa, I don't want to do this here. Not tonight.
It's your night. Your engagement party. We'll talk
about it another time.'

'No, we won't. We'll talk about it now. My best
friend and my brother are unhappy and angry and I
need to know why. I *deserve* to know why.'

Amy took a deep breath. She did deserve to know.
She told Willa everything else and she should have
told her about this. Maybe she wouldn't have cried
so much. Maybe she wouldn't have fallen for him the
way she had. Maybe her friend would have advised
caution and told her to hold back. And maybe that was
why she hadn't told her in the first place.

'It's just a disaster, Wills.'

The tears welled again in Amy's eyes but she
wasn't going to cry. Her eye make-up was on point
tonight and she wasn't going to ruin it.

She took another deep breath. 'We had a…a thing. It

was good. It was great. At least I thought it was. Then we went to Singapore and everything turned bad.'

Amy explained that she didn't think Luke had even wanted her there in the first place. How he'd told her about the guilt he felt about his mother and about Willa's divorce. She told Willa how they'd talked about Laurie and how she felt she'd let him down.

Amy fought back tears again when she explained how Luke had made her feel that night. Loved. Accepted. Normal. Then how he'd shut down and left her alone. She told her about their night in the office and their day on the yacht and how she'd thought that everything was good and they felt the same way about each other.

Then she told Willa about the argument, and how Luke had said that she was a wild animal and he didn't want a wild animal. And about how he'd looked her in the eye and told her he had responsibilities and that she had no idea what that meant. After spending weeks paying her attention and making her feel like the most important person in the world, it had taken one day and one argument for her to feel like nothing to him.

The tears did fall then, because she realised what she was so sad about. He'd never let her down before. He'd been there for her in her darkest time—he'd always had her. But that day on the yacht she'd felt that everything they'd had was a lie, and that was what cut her the most.

Willa listened without interrupting and without

moving. Then she breathed in through her nose and let it out, and took both Amy's hands in hers.

'Amy, I'm going to tell you something and I want you to know it's for your own good. Do you trust me?'

Amy nodded even while her heart pounded. She knew her friend. She knew that she was about to tell her some home truths and Amy wasn't sure she wanted to hear them. She knew it was over with Luke, but to have someone else say it would be terrifying. She wasn't sure she was ready for that.

'I've known you a long time, Amy, and I know what you're going to say and do before you even do it. I know that you sometimes act before you think. You speak without hearing. And I say this with love in my heart, Ames, but sometimes you're so busy trying to stay busy that you miss the most important things. You're a beautiful person, with a generous heart. You're quick to love and you're the most supportive and loyal friend anyone could ever have…but you never give anyone any *time*.

'Luke is the type of man who needs time. You can't rush him. He doesn't do well with snap decisions. And if he feels rushed, or pressured, or backed into a corner, he'll lash out. He says he's not a wild animal, but he is. Inside he *is*. He's spent most of his life being pressured into responsibility and doing the right thing. Then he meets you. And you do whatever the hell you want whenever the hell you want and *he* wants that. He wishes he could do that. And that's what frightens him about you.'

The tears were falling thick and fast now. Amy

gripped Willa's hands tightly. 'He doesn't love me, Wills. I love him. But he doesn't love me.'

Amy's words were soft. She could barely get them out. She knew she was being pathetic, but she'd kept it all in for so long now. It hurt. *She* hurt. She needed to let it out.

Willa took action. She pulled at Amy's hands until they found themselves in the ladies' room. Inside were two of Rob's aunts, reapplying their lipstick, and Willa swiftly asked them to leave. They looked peeved, but they did as they were told. Amy wasn't sure how she did it, but Willa managed to lock the door, and when she turned back she only said one word.

'Cry.'

But Amy couldn't. The tears had stopped. Her friend was here, she'd let it out, and she had nothing left.

'I'm okay…really.'

'You're not. You're a mess and it's my stupid brother's fault. Here.'

Willa opened her small bag and Amy peered inside. It was filled with make-up and tissues and Band-Aids and aspirins and everything else a girl could possibly need.

'Fix yourself up. Calm down. I'll be back in ten minutes. And then we're going to have a drink and celebrate my engagement and you're going to have fun and forget about my brother and the dastardly things he said and did. Got it?'

Willa was reserved and shy, but at times she could

be the strongest woman Amy had ever met. She nodded at her friend and they hugged the way only two girls in a bathroom could before Willa left her alone to fix herself up and prepare herself for a night of not thinking about stupid boys and their hurtful words.

Luke was angry. The man in front of him had had the hide to say New Zealand's batsmen were superior to the Aussies. Which was outrageous. Everyone knew that the current Australian line-up was the best they'd had in years.

'You've got no idea, mate.'

'Ha-ha—it's just a game, though, isn't it?'

Just a game? Who *was* this loser? 'If you think it's "just a game" maybe you shouldn't even be watching it.'

He stepped forward. This moron deserved a punch.

'Settle down, mate.'

'What did you say to me?'

Now he really *was* going to punch him.

'Okay, so everyone's happy here, are they?'

Willa had arrived.

'I think I need a drink.'

The moron left. Lucky. Because he'd been thirty seconds away from a piece of Luke Moore.

'Okay, Luke, I think that might be enough.'

'I've only had two beers, Willa, I'm not drunk.'

His sister raised her eyebrow. 'Not enough alcohol, but enough unprovoked aggression. You're going to drive all my guests away and then there'll only be you and me left here to party.'

'He was an idiot. Why do you always make friends with idiots?'

'I don't know, big brother. But I *do* know I'm related to the biggest idiot of all.'

'What?'

Surely Willa didn't want to pick a fight now? Not *now*. Not when he felt like this.

He hadn't seen or heard from Amy since they'd got back. She hadn't contacted him. She hadn't made any attempt to call him. She'd just walked out of his life as if the last three weeks meant nothing. Which was what he'd wanted her to do, so why the hell did it bother him so much and why the hell couldn't he stop thinking about her?

Everything reminded him of her. Smells, sounds, sights. It didn't matter what it was, he could come up with a story about how it was connected to Amy. He missed her so much. And it hurt. And he knew he couldn't have her because she didn't deserve someone like him. Someone who would let her down.

He turned to face the dark sky that was streaked with lightning. He waited for the boom of thunder. Five seconds. Five kilometres away.

'Luke. What's going on? You've been so angry and distant since you got back from Singapore. What happened?'

His whole life had been turned upside down—that was all. He'd let everything he wanted walk away—that was all.

'Nothing. I'm just worried about the Singapore deal.'

'Why? You said they approved it—what's to worry about?'

Nothing. She was right. Kel Huynh had finally approved everything. It was going ahead as planned, on budget and on time. That wasn't what was bothering him but he didn't want to tell Willa that. She didn't need to worry about him or anything else.

'You don't understand, Willa.'

He felt the punch on his arm and turned in surprise to see Willa staring at him, her eyes flashing.

'I *understand*, brother. I understand that you are an A-grade idiot. You let the woman you love slip away—and why? Because of some ridiculous guilt you have about our mother or me or something else you didn't do. There was nothing you could do about any of that. You couldn't save Mum. Dad couldn't save her. No one could. Then you took it upon yourself to become my keeper, which I didn't need you to do. I was fine. I had Dad. I had friends. I was fine. I *am* fine.'

'*Real* fine, Willa. You married an absolute loser and I did nothing about it. Don't worry, I've checked Rob out and I've let him know that this time around he'll have to answer to *me* if anything goes wrong.'

'I don't need you to do that! I'm not eighteen any more. I'm a grown woman. I can look after myself. I just need you to be my brother. To be there when I need you. The way you were there for Amy when she needed you.'

Willa's words felt like a punch to the guts. He hadn't been there. He'd let her down. Then and now.

That was why Amy had walked away. That was why she hadn't come back.

'As usual, Willa, you have no idea what you're talking about. Why do you think that thing happened to Amy that night? I saw them together. I *saw* that sleaze talking to her. I knew he only wanted one thing. And what did I do? *Nothing.* I walked away. I let it happen because that's what I do. I walked away from you, I walked away from Amy, and I walked away from Koko. And when I was lucky enough to get a chance to have Amy back in my life you know what I did? I walked away from that too.'

'Why, Luke? *Why* did you walk away?'

Luke stilled. Why *had* he walked away?

'Because he didn't love me.'

Amy's voice was like an elixir. His head moved towards the sound and he drank it in, and when he spotted her he drank her in too. She looked beautiful tonight. He'd spent the evening on the balcony, avoiding the chance of seeing her, knowing what it would do if he did see her. Knowing it would kill him to see her and not be able to have her.

'Amy.' It was all he could say.

'That's why he walked away, Willa. Because he realised that I loved him and he didn't love me back.'

It took a second for Amy's words to sink in. *What* had she just said?

'Isn't that right, Luke? You were okay with everything that happened between us until it came time to love me. You couldn't bring yourself to do that. Not silly, wild Amy. Someone you can't tame.'

'I don't want to tame you, Amy.'

'Then what *do* you want? Because I've spent the last five days trying to figure that out.'

He wanted her—that was what he wanted. But he was scared.

'You're just caught up, Amy. What we have—it isn't reality. It's fantasy. You know what would happen if we were together?'

'What? We'd fall in love and live happily ever after?'

'You'd be reminded every day of how I let you down.'

'How exactly *did* you let me down, Luke?'

'I let it happen. I let that bad thing happen to you. Then I hurt you in Singapore. I left you alone and then I hurt you.'

'You did hurt me. But you didn't let me down on Weeping Reef. That would have happened no matter what. If you had come over and tried to stop it I would have just been more determined. You know what I was like. And I was only with that loser to make you jealous. If you had reacted I probably would have done something even more unsafe.'

A beating started in Luke's heart. A steady thump that meant he was coming back to life.

'I should have stopped him. I should have beaten that loser before he had a chance to do that to you, not after. I should have kicked him off the island when he first arrived, not after he'd hurt you.'

Amy was silent and another crack of lightning lit the sky. One…two…three… Only three kilometres away.

'So Willa was right. You punched him?'

'Of course I punched him. I tracked him down and made sure he was sorry for what he did. And then I kicked him off the island. I watched him go. But I didn't stop it from happening.'

The lightning lit Amy's face as she came toward him. 'Thank you, Luke,' she said quietly. 'That was my only regret, you know—that I didn't say something to him. At the time, I thought he'd got away with it. I thought he'd stayed when I left and that made me feel like a victim. I didn't want to feel like that but I did—for so long.'

Luke watched her eyes. She was sad…he could see that. And *he'd* done that to her. He didn't want to make her sad. All he wanted to do was make her happy.

His chest filled with something that wasn't air. He wanted her close, holding on to him. Needing him. Not tamed, but still.

'Amy, I'm sorry.' He stepped closer to her, wanting to touch her. Wanting to reach out and pull her into his arms. 'I'm sorry I couldn't stop that. I'm sorry you got hurt. I'm sorry for the things I said on the yacht. I'm *sorry*.'

When she lifted her face the lightning caught it again. The boom of thunder came only a second after.

'I'm sorry I never told you that you were my hero that night. You saved me. You made me feel safe when I didn't think I ever would again. And now you're back. And you're saving me all over again.'

Lightning. Thunder. Then another crack and the

rain sheeted down. But Amy didn't move. She stood still and solid. His wild animal, looking up at him with her wild eyes. Soothed. Safe. All because of him.

'No, Lollipop—you've got it wrong. You're the one who's saved me.'

He reached for her then—he couldn't wait any longer. Willa had disappeared and everyone else had rushed inside as the rain started to fall. It was just the two of them and he needed to hold her close. He wanted to protect her from the rain and from anyone hurting her ever again. She was *his*. She was the most amazing, wonderful woman he'd ever known and he'd be damned if he was going to let her go. Not now that he had her back.

Slowly, but with confidence, he lifted a palm to her chin. 'Looks like I'm the damsel in distress and you're the knight in shining armour.' He smiled, and to his relief she smiled back. That slow smile he loved to watch creep over her face.

The lightning and the thunder cracked and boomed and the rain fell around them and over them. And all he wanted to do was kiss her. To feel her pressed against him. To feel her lips against his so that he knew where she was and she knew how he felt. He loved her and she loved him and they had each other and that was all they'd ever need.

'I guess we'll just have to save each other,' she said, and he knew it was time.

He leaned down and tasted the rain on her lips before she let him in. They kissed long and hard and deep, with the kind of desperation you only felt when you thought you'd lost something for ever only to find it again.

'I think we've wasted enough time, Amy.' He kissed her neck and her cheeks and then her mouth again as he murmured his words into her ears. 'I adore you. I love you. I need you.'

She broke away from the kiss for long enough to look into his eyes. 'Then this is the deal, Mr Moore. First you take me home and we make crazy love like the wild animals that we are.'

She smiled that gorgeous smile he couldn't get enough of.

'Then you marry me, forget about going back to Singapore, and we live happily ever after.'

His chest filled and his mouth smiled bigger and wider than it ever had. He'd never been more sure of anything in his life. He loved her. That was it. They'd met for a reason back on Weeping Reef, and that was so they could get to this point in time.

For the first time ever Luke believed in soul mates—because he'd found his.

'Deal.'

Then they sealed the deal with a long, deep, passionate kiss.

* * * * *

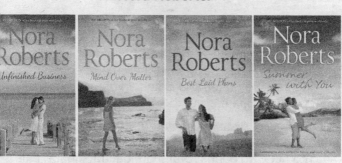

MILLS & BOON®

It's Got to be Perfect

IT'S GOT
TO BE
Perfect

UNCORRECTED
PROOF COPY

HALEY HILL

* cover in development

When Ellie Rigby throws her three-carat engagement ring into the gutter, she is certain of only one thing. She has yet to know true love!

Fed up with disastrous internet dates and conflicting advice from her friends, Ellie decides to take matters into her own hands. Starting a dating agency, Ellie becomes an expert in love. Well, that is until a match with one of her clients, charming, infuriating Nick, has her questioning everything she's ever thought about love…

Order yours today at
www.millsandboon.co.uk

MILLS & BOON®

MODERN™

POWER, PASSION AND IRRESISTIBLE TEMPTATION

A sneak peek at next month's titles...

In stores from 15th May 2015:

- **The Bride Fonseca Needs** – Abby Green
- **Protecting the Desert Heir** – Caitlin Crews
- **Tempted by Her Billionaire Boss** – Jennifer Hayward
- **The Sicilian's Surprise Wife** – Tara Pammi

In stores from 5th June 2015:

- **Sheikh's Forbidden Conquest** – Chantelle Shaw
- **Seduced into the Greek's World** – Dani Collins
- **Married for the Prince's Convenience** – Maya Blake
- **For Revenge or Redemption?** – Lucy King

Available at WHSmith, Tesco, Asda, Eason, Amazon and Apple

Just can't wait?
Buy our books online a month before they hit the shops!
visit www.millsandboon.co.uk

These books are also available in eBook format!